Perfect Strangers
Ballerina Laura Delgado is just one solo away from a dream job with the New York City Ballet. Then a drunken *pas de deux* at her cousin's wedding results in the one thing she never wanted—a husband. TV producer Charlie Laughlin may be deliciously kissable, but she needs him offstage now, and out of her life.

Perfect Disaster
Charlie's ready for marriage and kids, and on the lookout for just the right woman. Laura doesn't fit the bill at all—but Charlie can't stop thinking about the sultry way they moved together. And he can't help but wonder if he can change the gorgeous dancer's mind about leaving Miami with heated kisses that promise as much as they demand . . .

Perfect Partners
Annulling their sham marriage is all Laura wants—until she gets to New York and realizes that leaving Charlie behind is easier said than done. Can a relationship that began as a hot mistake become the kind of love that will last forever?

Visit us at www.kensingtonbooks.com

Books by Andie J. Christopher

One Night in South Beach
Stroke of Midnight
Dusk Until Dawn
Break of Day
Before Daylight

Published by Kensington Publishing Corporation

Before Daylight

One Night in South Beach

NO LONGER PROPERTY OF ANYTHINK LIBRARIES/ RANGEVIEW LIBRARY DISTRICT

Andie J. Christopher

LYRICAL PRESS
Kensington Publishing Corp.
www.kensingtonbooks.com

Lyrical Press books are published by
Kensington Publishing Corp. 119 West 40th Street New York, NY 10018

Copyright © 2018 by Andie J. Christopher

All rights reserved. No part of this book may be reproduced in any form or by any means without the prior written consent of the Publisher, excepting brief quotes used in reviews.

All Kensington titles, imprints, and distributed lines are available at special quantity discounts for bulk purchases for sales promotion, premiums, fundraising, and educational or institutional use.

To the extent that the image or images on the cover of this book depict a person or persons, such person or persons are merely models, and are not intended to portray any character or characters featured in the book.

Special book excerpts or customized printings can also be created to fit specific needs. For details, write or phone the office of the Kensington Special Sales Manager:
Kensington Publishing Corp.
119 West 40th Street
New York, NY 10018
Attn. Special Sales Department. Phone: 1-800-221-2647.

Kensington and the K logo Reg. U.S. Pat. & TM Off.
LYRICAL PRESS Reg. U.S. Pat. & TM Off.
Lyrical Press and the L logo are trademarks of Kensington Publishing Corp.

First Electronic Edition: April 2018
eISBN-13: 978-1-5161-0695-0
eISBN-10: 1-5161-0695-4

First Print Edition: April 2018
ISBN-13: 978-1-5161-0698-1
ISBN-10: 1-5161-0698-9

Printed in the United States of America

To Meya, Lucy, and Vayda. You don't ever get to read further than this page, but I love you.

Acknowledgments

I want to thank all of the readers who picked up the first three books in the One Night in South Beach series, and wanted more heat from Miami. The bloggers and reviewers who took the time read, review, and pimp my books rock so hard! I don't comment on reviews, but I read them, I learn from them, and I'm grateful for each and every one.

I would be remiss if I didn't thank Scarlett Cole for talking to me on Skype from across the world, and schooling me on how to be a badass author.

Thank you, Jennifer Herrington for making my words sparkle and shine. And being the best cheerleader ever. Thank you to the Lyrical marketing team, Michelle, Kimberly, and Lauren for helping me bring these books to the widest audience possible. Thank you to Martin and Alexandra for believing in this series.

Finally, thank you to my mom, who deals with the discomfort of reading dirty words penned by her daughter in order to be my #1 fan.

Chapter 1

Stock still, Laura Delgado stared at her Grandpa Rogelio with her mouth open. All the oxygen and all good sense in the universe had been sucked out of the room. Her dressing room had turned into the upside-down. Then, her knees gave out, and she dropped to the couch without meaning to.

Married!? My what!? The word *husband* echoed over and over in Laura's head. The two syllables sounded foreign and hostile. The disjointed—and altogether frightening—sounds reminded her of a Russian ballet master she'd once studied with. He'd thwacked her with a violin bow when she missed a step. The bow was less painful than the idea that she was actually married.

In her mind, marriage had always equaled death—a slow, painful, wasting disease suffered while handcuffed to the cause of death. And she'd just found out that she was terminal.

"Unless we get *his* signature, I can't file your taxes." *Two days from the deadline.* Her grandfather had the audacity to smirk at her as though he found this situation funny. He thought the fact that she was married and only found out about it...*funny.* If she didn't love her Grandpa Rogelio so much, she would be tempted to punch him in his still-handsome face. But, given that he was her favorite relative and he'd done her taxes without incident since she got her first paycheck from the company at eighteen, she just clenched her jaw.

And to make things even worse than the mere fact that she was married was the guy she was married to. *Charlie Fucking Laughlin.* With his artfully scruffy beard, his too-long hair, and naughty-looking mouth. He was smooth-talking and smug. Everyone loved him because he was so nice, but no one was that nice. Laura didn't like nice. Didn't trust nice. And now, nice-Charlie Laughlin was *allegedly* her husband.

She'd never intended to get married, and she certainly didn't picture ever ending up with someone like Charlie. He was too much everything—too handsome, too tall, and too sexy. By the time she was fourteen, right before she'd left home to join the ballet, she'd decided that she wanted nothing to do with marriage. Her parents had screwed it up enough to put her off the institution entirely.

There was no way she was going to end up tethered to someone like her father. Unlike her father, Charlie had a sense of humor, but he had the same charisma that her father used to try to control everyone around him. No way she was about to give herself no escape but the bottom of a pill bottle. Even though Charlie wasn't an emotionally abusive dick bag, he would end up trying to control her—he would want more of her than she could give.

How many Mai Tais—and how much tequila—had she had to drink? The only way she would have gotten married was if she'd been bombed out of her mind—or if he'd tied her up and dragged her down the aisle. But that would have left a mark.

If she had been on her guard, acting like herself, this never would have happened.

Images of a pink beach and matching pink drinks flooded her consciousness. The soft caress of the Indonesian breeze, the fuzzy joy at seeing her cousin, Carla, joyfully happy on her wedding day, and her disquiet at how much she *didn't* miss dancing during the three months she was out of commission from a groin injury slammed into her mind from the recesses of her memory. Since returning to the ballet, she'd stuffed thoughts of that night down so far that they exploded back like matter packed too densely in space.

But, every so often, her mind drifted to kissing Charlie at sunset, away from the crowd. It was the craziest thing she'd ever done—kissing a stranger. She couldn't get the feeling of his lips on hers out of her head. It was as though he'd stamped an impression on her, an invisible tattoo of his effect on her. Her entire life up until that point had been about discipline, training, dieting, and taking in criticism. She'd been a changeling at the behest of everyone in her life, and she knew that she could never let anyone know what was underneath her exterior. But there was something about the way he'd looked at her that had penetrated the wall she'd built around herself to avoid the pain of feeling she was never quite good enough, never quite the best. The feeling of his gaze on her skin—the feeling of him really *looking* at her—lingered along with the imprint of his mouth.

Either that, or she'd been so addled from the champagne toasts and tropical drinks that she'd lost her ever-loving mind. Crazy was the only thing that could explain how she ended up married to a sleazy reality TV producer who was once taped railing drunkenly about "bitches always breaking his heart." She didn't care that he was friends with her cousin and her cousin's husband. Well, technically, their employer—he produced an apparently non-sleazy reality travel show featuring her cousin, Carla, and Carla's new husband.

And he hadn't seemed like a slime ball at all when she'd seen him at the bar. But she'd married him. *What the fuck was wrong with her?*

Laura stood up and paced her dressing room, trying to figure out how to get out of this mess. She clenched her jaw. No one could find out she was married. If they did—if there was any hint that she was settling down—rumors would start flying that she was about to retire. Every time a principal dancer got married or pregnant, glee was a palpable thing in the rest of the company. Inevitably, a family and a serious career in ballet were untenable. At 28, she really should start considering leaving. The aches and pains that had annoyed her at 18 were nearly debilitating now. Most mornings, she had a hard time getting out of bed.

Nothing like waking up with Charlie—there she was warm and content. A totally foreign sensation.

An image of waking up in Charlie's arms, fully clothed, and cocooned in his warmth and the tropical breeze sent a shiver down her spine. And, even intensely hung over, she'd liked it. She shook her head.

If anyone in the ballet found out she had gotten married, the piranhas in the *corps de ballet* would start circling for her principal dancer position. And her chance to move to the New York City Ballet—to get a few years in the brightest spotlight in the world before retiring—would evaporate before they even came close to fruition.

"You can't tell anyone."

Her grandfather shook his head, not meeting her gaze. "Of course not." He would keep his promise because her getting married while drunk on tropical beverages and the romance of Carla's wedding to himself because it was embarrassing to the whole family.

He didn't say anything else, but his cheek twitched. Although he'd been around her a lot growing up, her grandfather was a cipher. She had very little idea of what went on in his head, or in his personal life. Her grandfather expressing an emotion would be almost as shocking as her father telling her he was proud of her or showing up to her parents' house and finding her mother sober.

Rogelio had moved to Florida with his two kids thirty-five years ago and rarely spoke of the wife he'd left behind. Since her Grandma Lola had moved to the States, she could see why her grandfather had never moved on. Lola was a force of nature who changed everything she touched.

She could tell that this situation was awkward for him. He'd seemed to inch toward the door after delivering the news. And all she had were feelings right now; disgust at herself, anger at the situation, and most of all—fear. "Seriously, no one."

"I'm required by law to keep our conversations confidential." Always the rule-follower, her grandfather. She got that from him, thriving on rules and routines rather than transient things like love. Though she'd been worried the return of her Grandma Lola would throw off the carefully balanced silence her family had come to over the years, apparently his ex-wife's return hadn't affected him at all.

"That's good." She turned away from himself. "Well, I guess you should file for an extension, *abuelo*."

* * * *

Charlie's back ached and his eyes burned. He'd spent over twelve hours in the editing room, making sure that the footage from Jonah and Carla's wedding looked just right.

Officially, they hadn't shot any of the intimate moments—the actual ceremony or the preparations, but they'd tied in part of the wedding to the shoot they were doing on different parts of the island.

But, for most of the night, until he'd gotten swept up with some very potent tropical drinks and Carla's fetching cousin, he'd gotten some footage of the whole family celebrating his best friend and his lovely bride. Carla and Jonah hadn't planned to have the whole family at their wedding; they'd planned to elope. But Charlie had not-so-accidentally let the cat out of the bag to Carla's great aunt, Lola, who had informed the entire Hernandez clan, which immediately threw them into action.

Carla and Jonah hadn't wanted to deal with the fuss of a big wedding, but now that his friend was finally happy, they deserved to have their family with them for their wedding. Charlie imagined that some military campaigns weren't carried out with the same precision as Molly Hernandez's wedding plans.

Charlie wasn't a stranger to big families—he had five brothers—but the Hernandez extended family made him feel alone even as they'd sort of folded him into the group. All of his brothers seemed happy doing their parts in the family business—television—enjoying all the wealth that came with it. They enjoyed the approval of their father.

Unlike him.

During his twenties, he and his father had butted heads so often over the shows Charlie brought into the network that every day had felt like a battle. And then, right after his very short marriage to his college girlfriend—which was an anathema in his family—had ended in her telling *TMZ* and the world that she'd left him because he was terrible in bed. Depressed, he'd posted a YouTube video of himself talking about how all women sucked. The video had gone viral, and he'd embarrassed his family. Even worse, he'd committed the cardinal sin in his family—he'd become part of the news cycle instead of dictating the news cycle from behind the scenes. The final blow had become when he'd been fired from the family business. He'd earned his reputation as a misogynist asshole with that video, and he'd tried to do penance since. He'd struck out on his own, and gotten out of the public eye. He regretted the distance between him and his family, but he was done being the family fuck up.

And despite the shadow of his shady past, he was happy with his life, or at least, he pretended to be. But in the past year or so, since Jonah had settled down, Charlie found himself wanting more. He wanted more than someone who assumed he was still that guy in the video. Someone who looked at him the way Carla looked at Jonah.

He didn't begrudge Jonah's happiness. His friend had had a long road to finding contentment with his wife and baby Layla; his college football career had ended abruptly and tragically after both his mother and girlfriend passed away. But Charlie couldn't help the pang of longing he felt whenever he was around Jonah and Carla.

Even though he'd been on a date almost every Saturday this year, Charlie had been having no luck finding someone who fit him as a long-term partner. Women either wanted him because they thought he would put them on TV, or they didn't take him seriously because he was a reality television producer. He made fluff. Too bad he was mostly attracted to women who thought the latter and never took the time to get to know him beyond the surface.

Women like Laura Delgado.

He rewound the footage until he saw her. His dick got hard just from the flash of her elegant neck and the side of her sharp jaw. The jaw he could still feel almost cutting into his palm as he held it still for a kiss. Getting Laura Delgado to let him kiss her had felt victorious. He wished they hadn't had so much to drink, and could have done more than kiss and frolic on the beach before falling asleep, wound together on a hammock.

When he'd woken up on the deck of his suite at almost noon the next day, partially cooked from sunburn, she'd been gone. Too bad, because he'd had plans for the lovely, prickly ballerina. And those plans hadn't faded away. If anything, they occupied more and more of his thoughts and his dreams. He'd never *craved* like this, and it was getting irritating.

Flashes of her gorgeous olive skin, her huge brown eyes, and that fall of thick hair tantalized him whenever his mind wandered. He felt like a crazy person wanting a girl he'd randomly made out with at a wedding so much that it was fucking with his sleep. He must have been living like a monk a little too much these days. All of his dating hadn't led to nearly enough sex; he needed connection for that he hadn't found with anyone but Laura.

When Carla and Jonah got back from their honeymoon, he was going to have to get Carla to give him Laura's number. Carla knew him well enough to know that his reputation didn't fit anymore. He had to see her again.

There was a commotion outside of the editing room where he was working that pulled his attention away from his stupid, dick-torturing memories. When the door opened, he could barely believe his eyes.

A very angry Laura Delgado, face red and breathing jagged, standing there and looking ready to kill him.

"You fucking asshole!"

Funny, he remembered her sounding sarcastic, bored, and a little breathless once he'd finally gotten her to put her mouth to better uses, but the thread of rage in her voice was new—and sexy. He tried to comb his mind for anything he could have done since returning from Bali that would have warranted this entrance and came up blank.

"What did I do?" He stayed sitting, certain he shouldn't make a move right now. His future ability to have children probably depended on it.

Her eyes narrowed into slits, and she slammed the door behind her. She wore a flimsy, cotton sundress, and he had to school himself not to give her the lazy once-over he was dying for. Somehow, he knew that flirting wasn't going to get him out of trouble this time.

"You did it on purpose, didn't you?" She walked toward him, her right hand forming a fist. The light shining from the screens cast part of her face in shadow, which served to make her look even more pissed off, like a cartoon villain. Was she actually going to punch him?

Confused, he held his hands up to cover his face. "I still don't know what I did."

She stopped about three feet away from him, and he was kind of glad. He was down for whatever sort of bedroom shit she'd like to do with him, but face-punching wasn't his kink.

"Are you just playing dumb, or are you just as clueless as I was until this morning?"

"Option B."

Her hand uncurled, and he finally breathed. She was still panting, and he wanted to offer her a seat, but she was a bit like a bomb about to go off right now, and he wasn't sure of the right move.

"We're married."

His brain flickered on and off like the lights during a thunderstorm. She couldn't possibly have said what he just thought she said. He looked at his left hand, wondering if a wedding band had suddenly appeared.

"When?"

She cocked her head and pursed her lips, regarding him as though he were an idiot. "When do you think, *asshole*?"

The "asshole" didn't have quite the same sting as the first one, so he guessed he was winning there.

"In Bali?" His brain was a complete blank. Embarrassment crept in over his confusion. He hadn't gotten blackout drunk since college. And, even then, it was once or twice. He even remembered making the stupid video, which was probably a big part of the reason Laura was so upset about being married to him. "I don't remember."

"Well, I don't either." She put her hands on her slim hips, still looking down at him.

"Do you want to sit down?" He gestured at the other editing chair, figuring she might need to take a seat. He'd have been on the floor in a very un-masculine dead faint had he been standing when she'd told him that they were married.

"No. I won't be here long."

"I think we have some things to talk about." Like divorcing him. *Fuck.* No one in his family but him had ever been divorced. That's not something Laughlins did. His parents would be devastated if he was the family's first *and* second divorces. He could imagine his mother's tutting over his failure right now. His brothers were all happily married and reproducing at an alarming rate—not him.

"I don't need to sit down for you to agree to an annulment."

Charlie shook his head, hoping to clear the cobwebs, but she must have taken it as a refusal to give her what she wanted.

"You're going to say 'no' to me?"

"No. I'm just—I'm just confused. How the fuck did this happen?"

She leaned over and he got a whiff of her scent. Fresh. Citrusy. He remembered that scent from burying his face in her neck and kissing up and down her pretty throat. Just that got his dick half hard, and he suppressed the groan that would probably bring back the fist.

"You. Tell. Me." Finally, she sat in the chair facing him. He looked at her face instead of her endless crossed legs. "I figure that you got me drunk and found the officiant because you knew that was the only way you'd have a shot."

Hard-on defeated. Anger, ready at the go. "Are you fucking kidding me?" It was his turn to stand up. "I would never do that."

"Well, one of the last things I remember was you telling me how much you wanted to get married, which I frankly thought was weird. And then, I told you that you were barking up the wrong tree."

Charlie didn't even remember that. He recalled walking over to Laura as she sat at the bar alone while everyone danced. He'd ordered them both drinks. Those fucking tropical drinks that had fucked his whole life up.

"The drinks—"

Laura moved her finger back and forth in his face. "Uh-uh. You're not going to pretend that this wasn't your plan all along."

He wasn't sure if the hair on his arms stood up because he was turned on or terrified of her. She was out of her damned mind, this one. "Why would I marry someone that I hardly know?" And someone who had made her clear disinterest in him plainly known as soon as he'd joined her at the bar. Charlie was an affable guy, a bit of a flirt, and they were two of the only single people at the wedding. He'd figured they'd have a drink and she could maybe make him look good on the dance floor.

She'd shut him down immediately, like before he could get a word out. Sort of like she'd shut down his explanation.

His shoulders collapsed, and he looked at the screen. He couldn't take the Laura Delgado death glare any longer. He wondered if she deployed it in order to get the best roles as a principal dancer. If she frightened Charlie with a flash of her fathomless, almost-black eyes, then a ballet teacher wouldn't be able to stand up to it.

He shook his head again, hoping to rattle a memory loose, some sort of clue as to how this had happened. "How did you find out?"

"My grandfather told me that he couldn't file my taxes without my husband's signature."

"So there's actual paperwork on this?"

"Apparently someone in the Balinese bureaucracy sent something to someone in the Dade County clerk's office, so we're all official."

Fuck. "I'll give you the annulment"

"Of course you will."

Her scoffing tone got under his skin—like the idea of marrying him was the worst thing that could ever happen to her. "What if I hadn't wanted the annulment?"

"We didn't consummate the marriage, so I don't think that would be an option for you."

She had a point. They'd both been drunk, but by the time they'd made it to the hammock, he'd had the presence of mind to put a stop to her digging in his trousers for his dick. Even with a long-term partner, drunk sloppy sex was not his favorite. And, with a stranger, it was completely out of the question. When they had sex—and the way their sparks were flying off each other, they would have sex—he wanted her present and willing.

Still, even though she was pissed at him and probably thinking of ways to detach his nads and serve them to him, he kind of wanted to consummate the fake marriage. Before she ended it. He wanted to kiss up and down her regal neck and unwind the tight bun so her hair would fall over and brush his chest. He wanted her to moan with pleasure like she had that night—their wedding night—when he'd rubbed her to a hard orgasm as a consolation prize for refusing to fuck her.

But, what he *needed* to know was how and why this happened.

And, he was sitting in the right room to do it. He hadn't made it to the footage of the reception yet, where any incriminating video might be found. If there was any moment to skip to the good parts, that moment was now.

Chapter 2

He had no right to sit there looking so good and smelling so good. Not while she was panicking and furious with him. The smile he'd given her when she'd stormed into the room was knee-weakening. And resolve-deadening.

"I was editing the wedding video while waiting for the Bali show to go through post-production. Maybe there's a clue as to how the fuck this happened here."

Laura couldn't stand how calm Charlie was about this whole thing. If she hadn't menaced him quite thoroughly when she walked in, he probably would have shrugged a shoulder, opened a beer, and moved on. This didn't even seem to register as a mild inconvenience for him. And, for some reason, that infuriated her.

She wanted him to act like a dick so she wouldn't feel guilty about yelling at him. He was being so accommodating and unruffled, despite the video he'd made about his ex-wife and her opinions about his sexual prowess five years ago. She'd watched it after Carla had told her about the television show, and her cousin had assured her that Charlie was not that guy. Jonah and Carla even let him babysit Layla, which spoke volumes about how much they trusted him. Carla barely let her own brother hold Layla—she'd told him that he needed at least five years free of stripper glitter before touching her. She'd been joking, but barely.

Delivering the news that his second marriage was about to be even shorter than his first kind of felt like kicking a puppy.

"Want to watch the tape and figure it out?"

That would be helpful, but she had to get out of this room before spending too much time with him. He was cute and helpful, and the idea of spending time with him—of him wanting to spend time with her even though she was completely broken—terrified her.

"I don't give a fuck how this happened. I just want it fixed." She had to stop being such a bitch. When she'd told him about the impromptu wedding, he'd looked just as shocked as she'd been when her grandfather had shared the news with her. This hadn't been a plot, just a terrible error in judgment. Even though a part of her was dying to know how they'd gotten from small talk to matrimony in a period of hours—or even minutes.

"Come on. You're not the least bit curious as to how we came to this state of wedded bliss?" He smiled at her, and she had to purse her lips to keep from smiling back.

She was curious, and needing to know when combined with his charm got the best of her. More than how they actually had ended up getting drunkenly married, she wanted to know how this had happened with her entire family around.

Because she could understand why someone would want to marry Charlie Laughlin—just not her. Just looking at him explained his marriageability. He was at least 6'3" or maybe 6'4" and had almost black hair and these arresting blue eyes. *Black Irish*, Lola had said. He was lean, and he clearly worked out—not as much as her, but no one worked out as much as she did.

But his fabulous looks weren't what made him so attractive, so disarming. Sure, part of it was the dimple and the mischief in his eyes when he'd looked at her. But it was more than that. When Charlie Laughlin put his attention on her, it was overwhelming.

When he'd looked up as she entered the dark editing room, she'd felt a punch of lust so powerful that it was even more maddening than the fact that she'd drunkenly married a very hot stranger.

And though she'd assumed he was a smarmy douche when they'd met before the wedding, none of that had been borne out by his behavior. He'd been editing his best friend's wedding video when she'd found him, not snorting lines of blow off various sex workers' body parts.

She could very well remember why she'd thrown off her strict diet and gotten drunk at the wedding—it hadn't been entirely clear that she'd be able to return to the company after her last injury anyway, so what was the point? And she knew why she wanted to kiss him—she liked the way his very kissable lips moved, and the sound of his voice made her hot and achy.

He was basically the human equivalent of the flu: contagious, debilitating, and possibly deadly.

While she'd been thinking about how dead sexy he was, he'd been fast-forwarding through video. He must have felt her gaze burning into the side of his face after a few moments because he looked up and said, "What?"

She shook her head. "I guess I'm still in shock. Can't believe I married you."

One corner of his mouth rose, revealing a dimple deep enough to stick her whole thumb inside. God, the editing room was cold. That had to be the explanation for her tight nipples and the goose bumps on her arms. And the reason her ribs felt tight around her lungs.

"Come on, I'm not so bad." His gaze returned to the monitor, and she felt like she could breathe again. "Some women even find me charming."

"I don't believe you." Her words had no fire because she found him charming, but she couldn't show it. She wasn't about to start showing weakness now.

She watched as he fast-forwarded the tape, stopping here and there. His hands were kind of beautiful. He had long fingers. Although he was way too rough and tumble to be a ballet dancer, there was something about him that moved with grace and economy.

Needing to stop looking at him, she turned toward the monitor, too. The tape revealed the sun diving behind the horizon, and she knew that the moment—if it was on tape—was coming.

Charlie stopped right at the moment he'd walked over to her at the bar. When she saw her own face, screwed up, trying to feign some imperious nature she didn't possess, her cheeks flamed. Her parents might have sheltered her from a lot growing up to keep her focused on her burgeoning ballet career, but they'd never taught her to be rude. And she'd been rude to Charlie. But something about him scared her, as though he was going to tip her apple cart right over and destroy the life she had built for herself.

She liked the way he looked too much—and he'd been even better in a linen shirt and pants that had shown his top-shelf ass. Not sure if it was out of embarrassment or a need to see that his posterior really was that distracting, she glanced over now.

Yep. Top. Shelf. Ass.

He just happened to turn at the same time, catching her. Her skin all over was on fire, and it made her feel like she was losing her mind. She was around gorgeous bodies all the time, and didn't have this reaction. Hell, men nearly as good-looking as Charlie had their hands right up near her business on an almost daily basis, and she didn't get to the same level of worked up that she was at right now.

Hastily, she looked back at the screen, just in time to see them do the first in now what she remembered as a series of shots. So many shots. And she couldn't even blame him for getting her drunk because she was clearly making a motion at the bartender for more. And more. And more.

"Can you fast-forward this?"

"No." His voice held a kind of bewilderment. "I need to understand how you didn't throw up."

"We can't know that I didn't throw up."

"Sure we can. I remember kissing you later that evening, and I clearly remember that you didn't taste like tequila vomit."

Laura only remembered flashes and scraps of kisses, and she suddenly felt like she'd cheated herself out of something special. She felt even more cheated when past-Laura grabbed Charlie's hand and dragged him out onto the dance floor. It made her downright salty to not recall the feel of his big hands with the graceful fingers all over her body as they swayed to a slow song. Past-her was such a bitch to be keeping all of those smiles and whispers and jokes that had actually made her laugh to herself. Past-Laura knew how to have fun, and past-Charlie had known how to give it to her.

She couldn't remember the last time she'd laughed. Because she certainly hadn't done much laughing since returning to work three months ago.

"Can you please just fast-forward?"

Charlie complied, and she was both thankful and bereft of the moments she was now deliberately, soberly ignoring. He stopped the tape again when they surrounded the officiant and dragged him into a corner. After a few minutes of what looked like tense negotiating, past-Laura, past-Charlie, and the officiant disappeared from the screen.

He stopped the tape and they stared at each other for a long moment, neither of them saying anything.

"Well?" She wasn't precisely sure what she was asking, never having accidentally married a stranger who happened to be a family friend.

"I can call Javi and see who handled his divorce." That wasn't a call that Laura wanted to make. Her older cousin would be discreet if she begged, but he would hold her shenanigans over her head if it suited him. "I think we can get an annulment because we were both drunk and we didn't fuck."

When she said the word "fuck," Charlie flinched as though she'd punched him. "I like that you're blunt, Delgado." He seemed to collect himself, and nodded. "Go ahead and call Javi. I don't want to pull in the studio's lawyers on this one."

"You have lawyers on hand for accidental weddings during shoots?"

The amusement was back in Charlie's gaze, and it immediately affected her below the belt. "No. We have had on-camera personalities and producers get into legal trouble, but the people we have on staff are business affairs guys. If it was someone else, I'd probably hand this over to them, but neither of us needs my mom finding out that I got married."

"Would you be embarrassed if your mom found out you'd married me?"

"I thought the whole point was that no one should find out?" He sighed, and clenched his jaw so his dimple made an appearance. "And I'd prefer it if neither of my parents found out about my second failed marriage."

She was surprised to hear him joke about it, and felt a pang in her chest. Getting married had been a terrible decision for both of them.

"Yes." She almost choked on the words because she didn't want anyone to find out, but the idea that she was an embarrassment to him didn't sit right with her. It probably sat about as well as her coming in here, guns blazing, demanding to know how he'd tricked her into marriage had less than an hour ago.

After that, they sat in silence for long moments. Very awkward silence. Finally, as she was leaning over to get her purse, he said, "Want to grab dinner?"

She wanted to say yes. It seemed like the right thing to do, the normal thing to do, grabbing a bite to eat with her husband, but she couldn't. Even this hour in the editing room was stolen from her true love—ballet.

"I can't. Rehearsal." He winced again when she said that. "Maybe some other time."

He stood as she did, like a gentleman. Though she'd stormed into this room, thinking he was the bad guy, he was a gentleman. "How about tomorrow?"

She had rehearsal tomorrow evening, too. Most tomorrows she was busy. A pang of regret roiled her empty stomach. She hadn't felt so much like she was missing out on a whole other life since she was a teenager. When other kids had gone to Friday night football games, she'd been at rehearsal. A boy from a local school had asked her to the prom, rehearsal. She hadn't even gone to a normal school, with days filled with academic classes. Academics were crammed in between rehearsals and performances, on road trips, and away from her parents and brothers.

Laura hadn't even realized that she was on her first date until one of the members of the company tried to kiss her after they'd shared salads after yet another rehearsal.

The idea of going to dinner with Charlie—a nice guy even if he weren't her husband—was so appealing to her that it had crawled into her bones. Which was why she had to shut it down and say no.

Ballet was the only thing she was good at. Outside of her family, it was the only thing she had. They had sacrificed too much for her to jeopardize it because she wanted something as silly as going on a date. Maybe getting to know Charlie Laughlin, a man who had gotten drunk with her and swept her off of her feet when she wasn't feeling like herself. A part of her she didn't let out very often, a part of her that she didn't know very well wanted to *remember* the full impact of kissing Charlie Laughlin. That part of her wanted to grab onto the one crazy thing she'd ever done in her life and never let go.

"I can't. We shouldn't." There. She didn't sound very strong, but she'd shut him down. She turned around to leave, not saying goodbye. She knew that if she said anything else, her no would turn into a yes in less than the space of a "see you around."

"I won't sign any annulment papers unless you go out with me."

* * * *

Charlie hadn't said a lot of stupid shit over the course of his life. He'd negotiated a whole hell of a lot, too. He was the guy his friends and his brothers called when they were in a tight spot because they knew he could bullshit them out of any hidey hole of trouble with his charm and quick words. And, if there was a woman involved, they called him with the quickness.

Still, when Laura had turned around and tried to leave, his wit failed him. Any other girl he would have been able to talk her into dinner after one of her rehearsals, but he'd smelled that for exactly what it was—an excuse. And he didn't know why it bothered him so much that she'd seemed to dismiss him after she'd gotten what she wanted.

He just knew that his gut twisted at the idea of never seeing the lovely ballerina again.

The idea that she'd walk out the door, file some paperwork, and be able to pretend that she wasn't the wild sort of thing he'd seen on screen a few minutes ago? That she wasn't the desirous and giddy woman he'd kissed and touched and held for one night?

Unacceptable.

Despite the reputation that he'd earned in the aftermath of marriage, he didn't make a habit of lying. But, as soon as she'd offered to get her family involved with getting this whole "oops we got married" thing fixed, he'd panicked a little, and a fib came out.

"We can't have sex, though." Her words were slow, as though she were talking to a small child. Funny how her mind went straight to sex when he'd been careful only to mention dinner.

"Why not?" He smiled, enough so that she would know he was teasing. If they had dinner, it would surely lead to the sex they hadn't had in Bali. There was too much—something—between them for it not to happen. He'd settle for a quickie with Laura if that was the only thing her schedule allowed. A hot, quick screw against the door of her apartment when he dropped her off after dinner probably wasn't as romantic as what would have happened on his ideal wedding night, but it got him excited almost as much.

"If we have sex, we can't get an annulment and we'll have to get a divorce, which will take longer and be more likely to go public."

"And that would be a bad thing." It definitely would be bad for him, and he would make sure it was good before. His ex-wife had lied about him five years ago. Sparring with her was giving him the idea that maybe an annulment was hasty. Perhaps he could convince her to give their marriage as shot. And, if she insisted on ending it, he at least wanted to enjoy his conjugal rights if his relationship record suffered another black mark.

For a few seconds, a moment ago, he'd thought that she was hurt by the idea of him not wanting his mom to find out they were temporarily married. Just a flash of something across her face that had hit him wrong.

"Yes." She crossed her arms over her chest, pushing her dainty breasts up. He couldn't not look. There wasn't much about her that he didn't want to look at.

"Why is it a bad thing? For you, I mean? My mother will lose her mind and light St. Patrick's on fire with the number of candles it will take to save my soul if we get divorced." Not to mention what he'd have to deal with from his father. He hated the sting of rebuke he felt from the man. His father was a lion of the business world. But, like male lions in the wild who killed their young, he only respected strength. Two divorces would stink of weakness all the way to Chicago.

Even more than he wanted to avoid censure from his parents, he wanted to know why she was so freaked out by the idea of marrying him. He stepped closer to her and her breath caught, making his dick go more than half-hard.

"Do you have any idea how competitive the world of ballet is?"

He'd thrown in the money for a web series on the American Ballet Theatre School in New York last year, so he had a fleeting understanding.

"A vague one."

She nodded and her lips turned into a thin line. "If word gets out that I've run off and gotten married, the piranhas will start circling."

"Who are the piranhas?"

"The *corps de ballet.*"

"Aren't they—like—your backup dancers?"

She let out a short laugh. "No, they're the enemy."

Charlie couldn't help but smile at the militant set to her jaw. Seeing her so worked up and passionate had him even more determined to get some time with her, to touch her velvet-soft skin and make her grit her teeth with pleasure. He rubbed the back of his neck, hoping to get ahold of himself. "I've gotta admit, your military metaphor kind of has me even more turned on."

She blushed and let out a huff of breath. "Of course, you don't understand."

"I understand, but there's no reason anyone has to find out that we got married."

"We don't even know how many people already know." The panic in her voice decidedly did not turn him on—in fact, he'd do just about anything to assuage it.

"We're connected through your cousin and my best friend. If we go out to dinner and someone"—he stepped closer to her—"sees us, they'll probably just assume that we're dating. You know? Like real people."

"I'm not real people." Again, with the school teacher voice that got him hard.

"Sure felt real to me at the wedding." He ran one finger over her forearm, and the electricity between them nearly set him on his heels.

The flush underneath her olive skin travelled all the way to her hairline when he said that, and he knew she was remembering what they'd done to each other. How shamelessly greedy she'd been with her kisses, how generous with her moans. He wanted that girl back, and he knew he could get her at dinner.

"Just one dinner." He smoothed a strand of hair behind her ear, almost feeling her heart skip with just that light touch. "I'd like to know a little bit about the woman I married."

"But no sex?"

That *almost* sounded like a complaint, but he was going to let it go. He didn't need to scare her off with the possibility that given some candlelight, delicious food, and his massive flirting ability, they wouldn't be able to resist ending up naked and sweaty—and in a very real, very consummated marriage.

He put two fingers up in a salute he remembered from the Boy Scouts. "Scout's honor."

Her eyes narrowed into slits, and he had to bite his lip to stop from laughing when she said, "You were a Boy Scout? Shocking."

"Why's that shocking?"

"It just seems so—wholesome."

"I'm a very wholesome guy."

"Yeah, a wholesome guy who marries a strange woman and sticks his hand up her skirt at a wedding."

"Hey, you called yourself strange, and I've only ever done that once."

"You did a pretty good job with the hand/skirt thing for your first time."

It was his turn to blush. "You've given me enough shit. Agree to dinner."

"Fine. Sunday night."

It might be the least romantic night of the week, but he'd take it.

Chapter 3

"*Abuela*!!!!!"

Laura's yell echoed through her loft condo. She'd lived with roommates—other dancers—until recently, when Carla, Jonah, and the baby had moved to a house together. Carla had called her up one day, asked a criminally low price for the condo and popped the keys in her mail.

A few days later, her grandma Lola had shown up with a suitcase and ensconced herself in the guest bedroom. Laura welcomed the time with her grandmother, who she hadn't seen much growing up. She'd had a convenient excuse because it had been difficult until recently to travel to Cuba, which Lola had refused to leave for decades after her children and ex-husband had moved to the mainland. But even if the borders had been open, Laura wouldn't have been able to spend school vacations in her ancestral homeland. She hadn't had school vacations; she'd had ballet.

Sometimes, when she returned home from rehearsal, she felt suffocated by Lola's presence. They didn't really know each other, and Lola had a big personality, the kind that swept a person up and set them down when it was good and done with them. Lola was like the twister from *The Wizard of Oz*. Except less predictable.

But tonight, Laura's condo was silent, and she was a bit a disappointed. If ever a girl needed her grandmother's good counsel, it was when she'd accidentally gotten married to a dashing stranger at a tropical destination wedding.

And then agreed to date him.

From what Lola had told her about her past, which was way TMI, it seemed like precisely the kind of situation that Lola had gotten herself into and out of plenty of times over the years.

Laura pulled one of her pre-cooked meals out of the fridge and turned the oven on to low heat. She'd hired a service to bring her nutritionally balanced, low-calorie food every week so she didn't have to think about it. Everything in her life was like that—suited and engineered to the life she'd chosen for herself. Looking down at her sad three ounces of salmon and par-cooked broccoli—no oil, no salt, no flavor—she wondered if it was worth it.

Seeing herself on that tape earlier, looking wild and carefree, was in stark contrast to how she'd felt later, at rehearsal. Dancing at her cousin's wedding, she'd looked happy. Thinking back, that whole weekend—far away from the company—she'd felt free. Rehearsing a new production of *Carmen*, she'd been scolded multiple times regarding her face. Apparently, she'd looked too sad to be a believable destitute sex worker. Her face was telling the story of being burnt out, tired, and sore all the time. It wasn't the kind of soreness she could shake off with a trip to the trainer, a massage, or even a frigid ice bath. It was the kind of soreness that told her she was approaching her sell-by date as a ballerina.

She was hanging on by her fingernails, and part of her wanted to loosen her grip and just let go. Maybe she could teach ballet or be a receptionist for her uncle, Hector, while going back to school. She'd need time to figure out the rest of her life. The possibilities seemed frightening and exciting at the same time.

She'd finished her meal by the time a key turned in the lock, announcing her grandmother's return.

"Where have you been?" She didn't intend for her question to come out as sharply as it did. Her tiny grandmother stopped in her tracks. Everything about her screamed color, from her flamingo-pink Capri pants to her azure-colored off-the-shoulder T-shirt. If Laura wasn't mistaken, there was pink in her hair.

"Out."

"Out where?" Laura didn't want her grandmother to feel like she was monitoring her, but she felt some responsibility for making sure her elderly relative stayed safe in a city she was just getting to know.

"None of your business." Lola certainly had the sullen teenager act down.

"Did you know that I got married in Bali?"

Her grandmother stopped in her tracks, literally froze in the middle of putting her purse down on the console table. The faint smile she'd had on her face while obscuring her whereabouts dropped, and her face took on an unmistakable mask of guilt.

"So you did know." A knot formed in Laura's belly. The idea that members of her family had been complicit in this foolishness made her want to scream. Her brothers and her grandparents had all been there. One of them certainly could have stopped her. Or told her about it before her grandfather had the chance. "*Abuela*, why did no one tell me that I'd gotten married?"

Lola had stepped fully into the dining area, and leaned against the back of the chair opposite to Laura's. "How did you find out?"

"*Abuela!*" Laura took a deep breath, trying not to lose her shit. The last thing she needed was to give her grandmother a heart attack. "Why did he know before I did?"

"We were going to tell you, *mi amor.*"

"When were you going to tell me?" Laura stood up to clear her plate, not wanting to look at Lola in that moment, but her grandmother followed her over to the sink.

"When the time was right."

Laura tried to focus on the water rushing over her hands, the slippery texture of the dish soap. Whenever she was upset about something, it helped for her to focus on what was right in front of her. She'd always been like that. As a little kid, she'd been all over the place, kind of a wild child. Ballet had given her something to focus all that energy on, and taught her to be present.

Right now, after finding out that her family had allowed her to make a colossal mistake, she felt like she was in a turn that had gone out of control. She was falling, and about to hit the ground, and focusing on the dishes was the only thing that would keep her from throwing the dish at the wall and shattering it into a million pieces.

"Who told you? It was Max, wasn't it? I may not know you children well, but I know—" Lola pointed up at the ceiling, as though she was calling on God for corroboration. "He has the biggest mouth."

"It wasn't Max." Her older brother might be the family communicator, but even he had been mum on the subject of her secret nuptials. "It was *your* ex-husband. I found out because he couldn't file my taxes without *my* husband's signature."

"I'm sorry."

Laura turned and looked at Lola, pressing her lips together to bite back the mean words that she wanted to say. Her grandmother appeared to be truly remorseful. Though she couldn't be certain if she was sorry for keeping the secret or the way that Laura had found out. "For what?"

"For not telling you."

"And you're not sorry for not *stopping* me?"

Lola shrugged and all the guilt evaporated from her demeanor. "You were having fun. Since I came back for Alana's wedding, I never see you have any fun. Charlie is handsome, and so I didn't pay close attention."

"Is that everyone's excuse?"

Lola took her hand and pulled her towards the living room. The older woman was shockingly strong, but Laura didn't fight it. She even sat down next to her grandmother.

"They didn't tell you because I didn't want them to tell you."

Laura gasped and balled her fists in her lap. "So you're the ringleader?"

Her grandmother then had the nerve to pat her hand. *Pat. Her. Hand.* "You looked so happy, and so—in love—the night of the wedding. I didn't want anyone standing in the way."

"How could I be in love with him?" Laura stood up, unable to stay seated in the face of such utter bullshit. "I barely know him, and I was drunk."

"How drunk?" Lola's brow furrowed, as though it was finally sinking in that she'd made a grave error.

"So, so, so, so drunk."

"I didn't know."

"So you thought I remembered all this time and had decided to say nothing about getting married?"

"I didn't *know* you really got married—legally—until you told me."

"You thought I had just gotten mildly tipsy and decided to have a fake wedding at my cousin's wedding with a guy I barely know?"

Lola stood up and shrugged again in a way that was growing more infuriating by the moment. "I didn't know exactly what you were up to, but I thought it was time you had an adventure."

"I don't need adventure, *Abuela*." She took a deep breath and turned away from her grandmother. "I need structure and discipline."

Lola made a haughty "pfft" sound. "The last thing you need is more structure. You work yourself into the ground. *Dios*, there's nothing to you but skin and bone." She walked around the coffee table until she was facing her again. Her face was soft, care dripping from her gaze. "You look so tired, *mi amor*."

"I'm fine."

Lola grabbed her arms. Laura's chest ached at the tenderness that she'd never really gotten from her aloof parents. They were broken people, and they didn't care much about how people felt on the inside. Her father had been too busy growing a business in a weird competition with her mother's cousin Hector when Laura was growing up to kiss boo-boos or even attend recitals. Her mother's answer for most things was an afternoon of shopping or a dosage of Valium.

Lola's tenderness, on the other hand, was palpable, and it made it difficult to stay angry at her. Even though she'd caused a major inconvenience for Laura.

She pulled away from her grandmother, unable to bear her pity. "I'll fix it."

"Can I help you?"

"I think you've helped enough."

* * * *

Laura was hoping that Charlie wouldn't pick a trendy restaurant for their first and last date. Her hopes were dashed when he called her and told her that he'd made reservations at Juvia, a trendy spot near the beach with a rooftop dining room.

Any hope she had of not being seen by any gossipmongers was dashed when he'd suggested it. She was sure he would have picked another place had she put her foot down, but she couldn't bring herself to do it. The notion that this wasn't a real date was dashed when she picked up the phone and heard his deep, raspy voice. He didn't even have to be in the room for him to affect her on a primal, physical level. She'd never felt like that before from just words, and it was disconcerting.

The man she'd married tested her hard-won equilibrium over the phone, but he blew it to smithereens when she walked out of her condo building to find him standing by a sexy, black sports car, wearing a suit that looked as though it had found fabric nirvana just resting against his skin.

Her husband was seriously sexy, which made it all the more imperative that he sign the papers folded neatly inside her handbag. She couldn't afford to let the warm feeling that overtook her whenever he was near steer her off course.

Not after all these years of sacrifice. Now that she was finally at the pinnacle of her career—or close to it—she couldn't afford to slide back down the face of the mountain. Because who would she be without ballet?

Probably someone like her mother, who had no passions of her own. Her mother had lived through her father's success. She hadn't done anything with her considerable intellect, and she was miserable. Her mother's misery filled her parents' house, and Laura could barely stand to be there. Half the time, she thought that the will to become a professional dancer had come from the sheer desire not to be at home.

And, despite the disparaging words from his ex-wife, Charlie was the kind of man that women threw away dreams for. Against that dark thought, Laura squared her shoulders and approached him as though he wasn't a walking live wire, ready to shock her carefully constructed life to death if she let him touch her.

"You look gorgeous." Such a cheap line that worked when it came from Charlie, with his pretty eyes and roguish smirk.

"I know." He gave her a full-on smile at that.

"Of course, you do." He opened the car door, and his hand went to her lower back.

She startled, but he didn't move his hand away. And she swore she could hear a sizzling burn from the touch of his hand through her filmy sun dress. It was God-awful hot this time of year, but the humid air wasn't the only reason she was sweating a half hour after getting out of the shower.

She took her seat, half to get away from his touch, half because she didn't want him to stop touching her. He must have just arrived because the interior of the car was still cool from air conditioning. Still, she wanted to fan herself to get the flush to leave her skin. One little caress and he had her heart beating as though she'd just rehearsed a solo piece for an hour. He got in and started the car again.

He looked over at her for a second when she reached toward the air vents to capture some of the cool air. Even that had a tinge of heat. She'd underestimated his appeal from the start, thinking he would be good for a fun night on the beach. A wedding fling. She hadn't realized that he was dangerous to her peace of mind.

"Are you hot?" He didn't keep the amusement out of his voice.

The problem with a guy like Charlie was that he snuck up on sexy. He was like a chili pepper that didn't hit the taste buds right away, but turned into a five-alarm emergency after thirty seconds of slurping up whatever it was in.

"It's 95 degrees and a hundred percent humidity." She glared at him, angry that he could see how disheveled she felt around him. He made her feel as though someone had ransacked her insides. "What do you think?"

"Aren't you used to that, growing up here?"

"I never spent much time outside as a kid."

"That's a shame."

She shrugged. "I was busy dancing."

"You sound sad when you say that." Irritation had her digging her fingernails into her palm, a habit she'd picked up to deal with jerky dance partners to prevent herself from yelling at them and risking one dropping her on her ass at the first opportunity.

"I'm not sad. It's the truth."

He moved his right hand to the top of the wheel, sort of creating a shield between him and her. She should like the fact that she'd put him on the defensive, but it disappointed her. Part of her wanted him to probe and find out more about her. She wanted to know more about him. Sure, they were getting an annulment as soon as possible, but she should know something about the man she'd married other than the fact that she was going to regret not consummating the marriage.

"Where did you grow up?"

"Just outside of Chicago." His body loosened, encouraging her to ask for more.

"Not quite as hot there." She looked down at her hands, not sure what she should say next. She didn't really know anything about this man, and she was curious as to why she'd done something so terribly impulsive with him. "What's your family like?"

He shifted his hands on the steering wheel again, and his body was more open to her. "Really normal."

She snorted. "What's that like?"

"Your family seems pretty normal to me."

"You haven't met my parents then?"

"No, just Mr. and Mrs. Hernandez."

"The Delgados are nothing like the Hernandezes."

"Really, how so?"

She paused, not quite ready to open up. "I asked you about your family. Tell me about normal."

"When I was growing up, my dad ran a newspaper, which is now a media conglomerate. All my brothers work for him."

"But not you?" Charlie's brow furrowed, and Laura wanted to run her finger across his forehead, smoothing the creases. She wanted to soothe him, but didn't know how. It wasn't often that she didn't know how to fix something.

"I didn't exactly meet my father's expectations."

"They were demanding?"

"Yes." He sighed and moved his hand as though he was about to touch her, but stopped and put his hand back on the wheel. They were close to the restaurant now; traffic had been mostly quiet. Laura had this feeling of time slipping away, as though she was about to lose an opportunity to really get to know this man.

"My parents didn't expect much." She said it, hoping maybe that if she showed him a bit of herself, that he would do the same. It didn't make any sense—this prying—but she had to know more about this man who filled her with delicious feelings, even though any involvement with him would be deeply inconvenient.

"But look at what you've achieved."

"It's not really *important*."

"More important than what I do."

"Maybe."

They both went silent, but she felt bad about him thinking that his work wasn't important. As a dancer, she often felt like something pretty and frivolous. A luxury, not a necessity. With previous boyfriends—few and far between as they had been—she'd felt like a trophy. Guys liked to say they were banging a ballerina, but they didn't so much like the long evenings alone. Every relationship she'd ever tried to start had stalled when the guys realized that ballet was her true love.

And she didn't dare date other dancers. The competition and vanity didn't make for anything healthy.

Sitting in the car with Charlie, talking about their families, felt kind of nice. Normal. She'd never even thought she'd get married and have kids when she was done dancing professionally. But the thought of it often made her feel as though she was facing down a prison sentence.

Normal for Laura felt like a punishment. From the few words Charlie had said on the subject of his normal childhood, they didn't see things so differently.

Chapter 4

Charlie wasn't sure where this date had gone off the rails. Maybe it was when she walked out of her front door, looking stricken by the sight of him. Her fear had thrown him. The last thing he wanted was for her to be afraid. Maybe it had been a mistake insisting that she go out to dinner with him before signing off on an annulment. She did look gorgeous, but she'd winced when he told her so. She seemed to be the only woman he'd met in the last few years who vexed him completely.

He had trouble forming whole sentences around her. His palms were sweaty, and not getting a hard-on when touching her lower back had been a feat. He was never this uncouth. After his ex told the whole world that he was a terrible lover, he'd tried to re-build his reputation. Never a dissatisfied customer.

But he had a formula, and he purposefully never talked about anything controversial. Nothing that could get too deep. And that was why none of his relationships ended up very deep.

He'd thought he liked it that way.

And then she had to go and ask about his family. The people who thought he was a commitment-phobic dilettante. His older brothers and his parents thought that moving to Miami had been all about putting off growing up. In reality, it had been the opposite. He wanted to settle down and have roots somewhere. But he didn't want his roots to be underneath the stifling canopy of being a Laughlin in Chicago. His father's reputation was so overpowering and lofty that it would always overshadow anything that Charlie did.

Her asking about them hit a nerve, and he was at a loss for how to respond.

Instead of trying and failing to make conversation during the rest of the ride to the restaurant, he brooded about his family instead. Laura sat with a serene demeanor, having no idea that she'd picked at something that had been bothering him his whole life.

His father's shadow didn't bother Jack, Danny, Sean, Jamie, and Michael as much. But it bothered Charlie. He wanted something of his own. And what he did might not be important journalism, but he liked the programs he was working on right now. He was letting people travel without leaving their living rooms.

He snuck a look at Laura through his peripheral vision. She was goddamned gorgeous. Elegant and utterly appealing. If she hadn't been drunk the night of Jonah's wedding, she never would have looked twice at him. She was the kind of woman who married a shady billionaire, not a bro from Chicago who owed his career to his dad.

He'd thought he would meet the right woman once he moved down here. Someone different from the women his mother thought he should be connected with—rather who his mother thought the family should be connected with.

He never thought he'd accidentally get married to a woman like Laura— gorgeous, talented, even Catholic—his mother would be over the moon. Except they weren't going to be married for long. She didn't want him, and that was a knife, deep in his gut.

When they got inside the restaurant, the maître d' showed them to a table near the corner of the roof. He'd asked for a private table because Laura had seemed hesitant about being seen in public with him. He'd wanted to bring her here because he'd heard her when she'd said that she didn't get many nights off, and he wanted to take her someplace special. He had to balance that against her desire to keep their brief marital affiliation private. Taking her out—even if that meant showing her off—had won out.

But when they sat down, it felt like a business meeting. Especially so when she reached into her purse and pulled out papers. Heat crept up his neck, and he clenched his jaw. This wasn't a real marriage, and he should be surprised that she wanted out of it as quickly as possible. Still, he couldn't help but feel rejected. He didn't have to feel that way very often anymore—not unless he visited his family.

He chose to ignore the gauntlet she'd thrown down, disguised as some folded up sheets of paper. Instead, he picked up the menu. "The food's good here. Do you like scallops?"

Laura ignored him and pushed the papers over. "You should look these over—have a lawyer look at them before you sign anything."

Charlie looked up and stared into her inscrutable, nearly black, gaze. "Do you have a pen?"

She didn't look away, but rooted around in her purse for a few moments, pulling out a black pen. He placed the menu carefully over his table setting, wanting to toss it instead. He opened the sheaf of papers, aware of her watching him the whole time. Not taking the time to read the document, he signed and dated the bottom and pushed them back at her.

He didn't know why it bothered him so much that she'd brought the annulment papers out to dinner. In fact, he'd kind of expected it. She didn't want to be married to him. They didn't know each other, and he could almost feel her disdain toward him in the air when they were together. There was just some part of him that wanted to tap back into the kind of passion she'd had when she'd let go and danced with him the night of the wedding. He wanted more of that reckless abandon, that unfettered lust. Despite her cold exterior, he had the feeling that the woman he'd met in Bali was more of the real her, and he might be the only person who cared to coax her out.

The icy ballerina served everyone else—the ballet company, her family, even the dancer herself sometimes. But he couldn't shake the notion that she'd zeroed in on him for a reason, goaded him into doing shots with her for a reason, married him for a reason. He just had to keep her hanging out with him long enough to find out.

"So, do you like scallops?"

* * * *

"You should really look that over carefully." For a moment, when he looked at her over their annulment papers, she'd thought he wouldn't sign them. There'd been so much anger and hurt in his gaze that guilt had rolled her stomach for a second. And then he'd signed them, pushed them away as though they were distasteful and asked her what she'd wanted for dinner as though nothing had happened. It was as though the pain shining out of him no longer existed.

He wanted to act like this was a normal date?

"Why do I need to look them over carefully? Did I just sign over a kidney?"

"No, we each keep what's ours."

He looked up from the menu again, this time a crooked smile on his face. His mouth was so fucking sexy. She wanted to taste him again. Wanted to pull his full lower lip in between her teeth and know she had him at her mercy. She wanted to roll around in the smell of him and fuck him. She'd never been quite so *driven* by the need to fuck as she was when she was around Charlie. She was a physical person, and he was objectively gorgeous—simply a well put together human—but there was something about him that drove her absolutely crazy.

She could almost understand marrying him impulsively if she were anyone else, if she hadn't trained the spontaneity out of herself with brutal, ruthless precision.

When she didn't stop looking at him, he winked at her, and her sex flooded. He was lethal and she would do well to forget it. She would have a nice, civilized meal with him. Keep it light—first and last date talk—and go home. She might run into him if she was hanging out with Carla and Jonah, but she didn't *hang out* so her exposure to him would be limited.

She cleared her throat and looked down at her menu. Everything looked delicious. She wanted to order everything and take a bite of each dish. But that would be decadent, and she doubted her *pas de deux* partner would appreciate the overindulgence at rehearsal tomorrow. So she went forward as she hoped to move on with someone as scary-sexy as Charlie, she stayed safe.

"I think I'm going to get the salmon."

* * * *

It was the worst first date that Charlie had ever been on. Awkward silences, stilted small talk, and an overly attentive server who had the gall to flirt with his date set his teeth on edge. Of course, the waiter recognized Laura. Being a ballerina was not like being a pop star, but she was a principal dancer and gorgeous to boot.

He really shouldn't blame her for indulging the guy, but he wouldn't fucking leave them alone, stomping all over his last nerve. But Charlie couldn't help but want her to smile at *him* that way. There was no way he could charm his wife into dating him if she refused to pay him any attention.

The only saving grace was getting to watch her eat. He'd been prepared for her to complain or order something boring and healthy off menu, but surprised him. She made noises when taking the first bite and the second which curled around his dick like one of her soft hands, making it hard for him to breathe.

"Is something wrong with your dish, sir?"

Charlie shook his head, hoping to clear some of the filthy shit in his head. "No. It's delicious."

He put another bite of steak into his mouth, but it tasted like nothing compared to the memory of almost having Laura Delgado. Of having her panting and moaning and begging for him to finish her off. He wondered if she would let herself go like that again, or if Bali was a one-time thing. He wondered if she could give herself over, or if she'd suffered the same temporary insanity that had taken him.

Finally, after what felt like an hour, the waiter left to see to his other tables.

"Why are you so grumpy?" Laura winked at him. "I agreed to have dinner with you, didn't I?"

"Yeah, you agreed to have dinner with me." Why was he being such an asshole? He wasn't usually an asshole. Or, at least he tried not to be. "Not the fucking waiter."

"Jealous?"

"And if I was?" He looked at her purse, where she'd tucked in the annulment papers.

"You're not my *real* husband."

Of course, the waiter picked that moment to come back and refill their waters for the umpteenth time. The way he stumbled and just saved himself from spilling ice water all over their food gave it away. Along with his red face.

Laura blanched and Charlie's collar seemed to tighten although he had the first two buttons on his shirt undone. They all stared at each other in a long, awkward silence.

"I'll have another glass of wine, please." Her request surprised him. He would have expected her to cut their evening off right there. Instead, she was volunteering to spend more time with him.

"Right away Ms.—ahem—Mrs."

"It's just Ms." Laura flipped her hair over her shoulder in flirty gesture towards the waiter. "And he's not my husband."

He completely understood what she was trying to do, and he ought to have backed her up. But he hated her saying that he wasn't her husband.

"Whatever you say."

After the waiter hurried away, Laura turned off all that flirty light she'd been using on the other guy. "This is why having dinner was a bad idea."

"Seriously, why is it so bad that some guy thinks you're married to me?" Charlie honestly didn't get it. It wasn't like she'd be the only married dancer in the company. After she'd stormed into the editing room, he'd done some research. One of the other principal dancers—the guy who partnered

with Laura most often according to the website—was married, too. And
to a man, so Charlie felt a little less jealous about his hands all over her.

"It's just a bad time for me in my career for this to happen."

Maybe she was worried because she didn't remember the wedding
night? Maybe she thought that he'd lied to her about that?

He guessed the evening couldn't get any more awkward, so he ought
to clear it up. "Nothing happened the night of the wedding. You're
not pregnant."

Again, she blanched. "I didn't think I was." She sighed. "But the
possibility that I could be. That I could even be thinking about it is enough
to doom my career."

"Everyone raves about your performances." He gestured towards the
bar, where the waiter was presumably fetching her wine. "The waiter was
practically singing you an ode earlier."

She looked down before saying, "But I want more."

"What do you mean?"

"I want to move to New York. I want to dance for the New York City
Ballet before I retire."

"New York sucks." Charlie hated New York. On principal because he
was a Chicagoan at heart. And practically, he hated how crowded and
impersonal the city was. He much preferred Miami, with its color and more
chill vibe. "Why would you want to live there when you could live here?"

"But it's the best company in the country, and I've always wanted it."
She threw down her fork, and it rattled against the plate. "Haven't you
ever wanted more? Better?" He'd moved here because he'd wanted to
prove something—to his parents and himself. He'd wanted to get out from
underneath the shadow cast by his father's reputation and build something
of his own. Moving to New York he could have done that. But he'd wanted
something smaller, that he could control without having to take heart
medication. He didn't want a sprawling media empire; he wanted freedom.
But, based on what she was telling him, she wanted bigger, brighter lights.

Disappointment made its way through his system, and not for the first
time that night. He'd expected the date to be fun and light. Instead, she'd
just revealed the core of why the two of them were doomed before the
accidental wedding—they wanted different things.

If he were a mature, sane adult, he'd pay the check and drive Laura
home. He'd call her next week and make sure the papers were filed without
problems and pretend that none of this ever happened. She'd move to
New York, and he wouldn't see her for a few years. By then, this whole

sham marriage would be a faded memory. Hell, maybe they'd be able to laugh about it.

But part of him wouldn't allow him to do the adult thing. He *wanted* Laura, wanted to be around her. It was inexplicable and irritating because she clearly didn't feel the same way. Though, his dick and maybe his heart wouldn't take her reluctance for an answer.

"I want more with a lot of things." Her. He wanted more with her.

"And I'd bet you don't let anything get in your way when you want those things."

She had him there. "Nope."

"And you don't want to stand in the way of me getting what I want, do you?"

He was totally honest with her—if not with himself—when he said, "I want you to get everything you want in life."

She gave him a beguiling half-smile. "And if I can't get that because I married you?"

"I'd feel terrible about that, and that's why I signed those papers."

"But you're not happy about it."

The air changed between them when she left those words hanging there. No, he wasn't happy about annulling the marriage. He was man enough to know that it was the right thing to do, but his ego was fragile enough to chafe at the fact that this girl didn't like him.

She was right, he was a driven guy, and he always got what he wanted. He just appeared to be laid back about everything. There was more of his father inside him than he'd ever admit out loud.

She saw right through him, and that's what got him about her. He'd always loved women who gave him shit; there was no better way to get his dick hard, if he were being completely honest. And this woman didn't even let him get away with polite shit when it would be appropriate.

So, he decided to push her back. She thought she knew his MO, but she was wrong about him. If only he had the chance to show her that. They connected on a sexual level, and maybe that was something he could work with.

"No, I don't like it." He shrugged, trying to seem cool. "I'm kind of disappointed that I'll never get to fuck my wife."

Chapter 5

Laura choked on her wine. It went down the wrong pipe and she coughed until the people around them stared at her. Charlie got up and rounded the table, patting her back and rubbing—a gesture both soothing and menacing given what he'd just said to her.

"I'm fine."

He stopped the rubbing, but he didn't move his hand. "Are you sure?"

Not really, but she said, "Sit down. You're mortifying me."

That made him move his hand, immediately. "I just wanted to be sure that you were okay."

"So that you could maybe fuck me?"

He smiled and she scowled in return. "I've got you thinking of the possibilities, then?"

"No."

"How much do you remember from the night of the wedding?"

More than she'd ever admit out loud. After seeing the video, a lot more about the rest of the night had bubbled up. She remembered kissing, touching, asking for more. Frustration that he wouldn't go all the way. She'd embarrassed herself trying to push him further. And the memory now flooded her with heat and longing for something it would be stupid to ask for.

Even if he wanted it, too.

"I remember enough to know that we don't need to go any further."

"I disagree."

"Do you ever take no for an answer?"

"No." He swirled the last of his one glass of wine before downing it. "Do you ever say yes to anything that isn't already in your life plan?"

"No." At least not before now, when she desperately wanted to say yes to an affair with Charlie. Despite the fact that they didn't have much to say to each other, he was gorgeous. And his touch against her skin made her nerves dance. It wasn't love, but it was lust. It was connecting to a feeling when she hadn't been sure she hadn't lost the capacity to feel long ago.

"Listen, I think there's a reason you sought me out at the wedding. And there's a reason you drank too much." He lowered his voice to a course whisper that rasped along her skin like a lover's touch. "And there's a reason you married me."

She leaned back in her chair. "What do you think that reason is?"

"You're not sure about your path."

Even though deep inside she knew he might be right about that, she wasn't going to admit it out loud. "What makes you think that?"

"I know that when I want something, I'm not going to risk fucking it up by losing control." That statement made her curious to see what Charlie would be like if he ever truly lost control. "And I think we're the same that way."

"And you think us fucking will clear my mind? Convince me to stay here in Miami?" To live out the rest of her career—which was growing shorter by the day. And then what? Teach classes at local studios? What would she do with herself without the discipline of pushing herself ever further? Turn into her mother, and that was maybe the scariest thought to ever cross her mind.

"No." His face changed; his whole energy shifted from a man trying to convince a woman of something to a man who knew he had a woman convinced. "But I think it will be fun, and you deserve some fun."

"But if we do this." She motioned between them. "Then, we can't get an annulment."

"The way I see it, the papers are signed." He reached across the table and took the butter knife she hadn't realized that she'd been clutching out of her hand. "And neither of us is dumb enough to tell a judge that we actually consummated the marriage. This wouldn't be part of the marriage that never happened. This will be part of the affair we should have instead."

He sounded so fucking reasonable. And him touching her was convincing. Maybe she had hit on him and plied him with alcohol because she wanted to let loose. She'd never done anything like that before. Her entire late adolescence and early adulthood had kept her wrapped up tight. Even if she hadn't left home to stay at the academy during her high school years, she doubted her parents would have put up with any public misbehavior.

Charlie was presenting an opportunity to live a portion of her life that she'd skipped. This incredibly gorgeous, enticing man wanted *her*. She wasn't a stranger to being an object of desire, but this was something else. Behind whatever image he cultivated, there was an intensity that pulled her in, even as she feared that his attention would pull her under and make her dreams of reaching the pinnacle of her career less compelling.

It would be a dumb move to get along, but she couldn't quite get herself to say no. "So, we go home from this frankly mediocre date and have sex?"

"I was thinking we could try the whole date thing again."

"Why do you want to date me?" It didn't make any sense. "Or, are you just an entitled asshole who can't stand taking 'no' for an answer?"

"I am an entitled asshole, but I can accept rejection."

"Then why won't you let this go?" She was irritated, yes. But it was more curiosity at this point that was keeping her from leaving the restaurant and hailing a car. "What is it about me in particular that you can't accept a no from?"

He shocked her by running a finger over the back of the hand she had laid on the table. It sent waves of something through her body that seemed too big for her to call lust. "Do you need me to tell you how gorgeous you are?"

She didn't need that and just raised her eyebrows in response.

"You don't need me to tell you that. People tell you how beautiful you are all the time. The issue is that you're more than beautiful. You're compelling and a little bit mean. It makes my dick hard when you lift that aristocratic nose at me."

"So, you're saying I'm a challenge?"

"Not just a challenge."

"What then?" She could barely breathe waiting for him to say the next thing. He seemed so angry about having to articulate why he wanted her, as though he didn't want to want her as much as she hated the heavy fog of lust he pushed her in to whenever he touched her.

"You're just different from any other woman I've ever met. I hate the idea of you leaving Miami, but I get your ambition. I understand the need to get away from your family and everything you've ever known. I think we're a whole lot more alike than we are different. And I just—I want to explore that."

"I haven't felt this way about someone else either." She hadn't wanted to say that, hadn't intended to, but she couldn't help herself.

"How do you feel?"

She took a sip of wine, squaring herself up. By nature, she was not an effusive person. She was calm and calculated, disciplined. Ever since she'd started dancing, she hadn't been prone to outsized emotions; she'd channeled all of it into her art. Feeling overpowering lust for a person rather than a piece of choreography was new to her.

"I feel like you see me when you look at me." She took a deep breath. "You don't see the dancer, and you don't accept that I'm as cold as I try to make people think I am."

"Why do you do that?"

"Because it's better than the alternative."

He leaned forward, and even across the table she could feel the space around her closing in. "I'll keep your secrets about the non-marriage. And I won't let anyone know that you aren't the hard-assed bitch that people think you are."

"Then I guess I owe you another date."

* * * *

Laura's second date with Charlie hung over her head like a sword of Damocles for the next week. The only good thing about that worry was that it took her mind off how poorly rehearsals for *Carmen* were going. She'd danced this ballet numerous times, but this time something was off. And she couldn't even discern the problem, much less figure out how to fix it.

She and her partner were rehearsing the climax of the ballet, and they'd been at it for hours. Every time they ran through the steps, a hand would slip or be in the wrong place, the lines of their bodies would be off. She was lucky that he hadn't dropped her multiple times.

Finally, the choreographer for this new version of the ballet stopped them and told them to take a break. He said there was a sponsor coming in that he needed to greet, but she knew it was an excuse not to have to look at them any longer.

Disgust with herself flowed through her veins like a familiar drug. She had a tolerance for it, given her perfectionism and profession. And she fought mightily to keep it from pulling her into full-on self-hate. A lot of younger dancers ended up with serious eating disorders because of the demon-drug of perfectionism that they all imbibed. She'd never been one of them, and she'd always viewed her body as a machine that needed fuel. Her dancing had never improved through a diet—only more practice.

And now, it wasn't helping. She and her partner sat with their backs against the wall under the barre, breathing heavily and gulping water. Her leotard was sticky against her skin and soaked through with sweat. She smoothed back tendrils of hair that had escaped the severe bobby pins and bands that kept her hair in place.

"What's going on with you?" John, her partner, asked. She wouldn't call him a friend, exactly. She didn't really have many friends other than her cousins, but they were friendly acquaintances.

"Not sure." John pressed his lips together. She was usually a reliable partner, and he was clearly getting frustrated with her. Guilt for fucking this piece up surfaced.

"How's your groin? Still aching?"

Yes. The answer was always yes, but she would never say that out loud. "It's fine. Completely healed."

"You know, you don't have to pretend it doesn't hurt." He put his hand on her shoulder, and it felt comforting. Also patronizing, but comforting just the same. "We all hurt."

The door to the studio opened again, and Charlie walked in with Matthieu. Everything became sharper, the sweaty leotard, John's heavy hand, and the air against her skin. When Charlie looked at her, all the blood in her body seemed to pool at the apex of her legs and her nipples. She wasn't sure why seeing him here—having him walk into this room—made her feel so aware of him. Perhaps it was the shock of seeing him on her turf. Or maybe it was just Charlie.

He was just as devastating in today's suit as he'd been at dinner. Today, the shirt was crisp white and the suit was black. It hugged his shoulders like a lover. His unbuttoned jacket revealed his flat stomach. She couldn't help herself but look lower from her vantage point on the floor. And apparently, he was free balling. Her skin flushed and she looked up just in time to see his reaction to her.

His gaze narrowed when he registered John's hand touching her bare skin. Instinctively, Laura moved away, standing up, less gracefully than she normally would.

She was unsteady on her toe shoes, and it was only when he leveled a panty-melting glare at her that she squared her shoulders and approached him.

The choreographer, a man who she'd worked with multiple times, put his arm around her. She thought Charlie's eyes would bug straight out of his head. And she didn't miss his fist bunching when Matthieu kissed her cheek.

"Mr. Laughlin tells me that you two have met."

Good thing she hadn't eaten anything in several hours. She would have choked.

"Yes. Briefly."

Charlie finally took his gaze off of where Matthieu touched her. "I'd say it was more than brief." She opened her mouth to issue a denial, but he cut her off. "I'm a friend of the family. We met at a wedding."

Matthieu, having no clue what was going on and that the two people having a conversation around him were plotting ways to kill each other slowly in their heads. At least, that was what Laura was doing. Charlie was probably still trying to figure out how to sleep with her.

"What are you doing here, Charlie?" She tried to keep her voice light, but her gritted teeth probably gave away her consternation.

"I'm sponsoring the ballet."

Her stomach dropped out of her body and the room started to spin. He thought he could buy her? If he did, he had another think coming and coming fast. He didn't know her, didn't know that the idea of a man owning any piece of her was a soft spot born of the family she'd grown up in, but he was going to know this soon.

But not now because they had an audience.

She managed not to fly across the few feet between them and wring his neck. She even managed a semi-polite response. "I didn't know you had any interest in the arts."

One side of his mouth quirked up, as though he knew that she was about to strike out at him like a viper. Maybe she had a vein popping out of her forehead that she couldn't control. "Interest in the arts? I work in the arts."

"I wouldn't call what you do art."

She felt Matthieu's shock in the way he squeezed her shoulder. "She doesn't mean that."

"Of course I mean it." Laura shook off her friend's touch, and Charlie's posture loosened immediately. "We're *friends*, and we've already discussed how I don't like what he does." She stopped, her gut twisting into knots at the terrible notion that Charlie wasn't sponsoring the piece out of the goodness of his heart, but a desire for access to the behind-the-scenes world of ballet. "He's not going to start taping rehearsals, is he?"

"We hadn't discussed that." Charlie's answer didn't make her feel any better.

Laura turned to Matthieu. "Will you excuse us for a moment?"

Her friend opened his mouth, probably to say no for the good of his employment and his piece. But Charlie cut him off. "I get a private audience?" He put his hand over his heart, and it reminded her of how even incidental touches from this man set her whole body afire. Being alone with him was a bad idea. He was her new patron saint of bad ideas. "I would be so honored."

His sarcastic tone burst the bubble of lust in her belly, and she grabbed him by the biceps and dragged him out of the room. She wouldn't have been able to do it if he had resisted, and he should have resisted for the sake of his balls.

Once they got into the hallway, she rounded on him. "What the fuck are you thinking?"

"Why are you yell-whispering?" He was purely amused.

"Because anyone... *Anyone* could walk by, and I don't want them knowing that I committed murder to keep you quiet."

"What's the big deal?"

"This is how you keep our—*association*—on the down low?" That one came out as a shriek.

He shrugged and smiled. The smug bastard. "I figure that this is a good cover."

"No. It's not." She pointed a finger in his face, and he grabbed her whole fist in his hand.

"Watch it, gorgeous."

"Don't tell me what to watch." That didn't make any sense, but it was emphatic and got her displeasure across, which was the point right now. "You need to leave. Take it back. And I don't want to see you again."

"Until we have dinner with Carla and Jonah next week?"

She yanked her finger back, and tendrils of frustration disguised as rage worked their way through her. "You're not invited to that."

"Yes, I am."

"Consider yourself uninvited."

"No."

This man was going to be the end of her. "Go grab beers with Jonah some other night."

"No. I'm not going to see Jonah. I'm going to hang out with the baby."

"She goes to sleep at seven. Dinner's at eight."

"I'm going over early."

"Well, leave before I get there."

"No." He leaned down and put his mouth close to her ear. Her body, already flushed from rehearsal, nearly overheated at having him so close. "And if you put up any more of a fuss, I'm going to tell your buddy Matthieu that he needs to keep his hands off my wife."

"You wouldn't."

He cocked his head in response. Before she could get any choice curses out, he ran his hand over her bare arm and cupped her elbow. It was chaste, friendly even. Nothing overtly sexual about it. But it was as though he'd run that hand between her legs and wiggled it under her leotard. Goose bumps rose all over her skin, and heat pooled in her belly so fast, she probably needed to change leotards.

"Have you even filed the papers yet?"

The answer was no. She should have sent them over to her grandfather the day after Charlie had signed them, but something kept her from doing it. Standing here, facing off against him, made her realize that this energy between them wasn't going to go away. This heat that flared up whenever he was in her space was something more powerful than she could wrap her mind around. It was so compelling that she couldn't bring herself to make the final step and push him away for good.

She'd never had a hard time making the logical decisions that would get her where she wanted to go. No one who knew her would guess that she ever hesitated about making the logical choice about anything. But damn her, standing here looking at Charlie and the way he filled out a suit, smelling the soap he showered with, and feeling his gaze raking over her as though she turned him on twice as much as she pissed him off, it didn't seem logical to not want to be married to this man at all.

But she couldn't tell Charlie that. Couldn't let on that he had the upper hand with her, especially now that he literally had the upper hand by sponsoring the ballet.

She never wanted to see Charlie again—it was bad for her sanity—but it didn't appear that she was going to be able to avoid it at least one last time. Unless she ovaried up and gave the papers to her grandfather.

"I hate you."

Then, in a move likely designed to make her head blow up, he kissed her cheek. His fresh spice smell and warm dry lips were custom-made to make her nuts. As impactful as his touch was, it was gone just as quickly as it had come.

She was left standing in the hallway, shivering now that her sweat had dried and Charlie's heat was gone, staring after him.

And, damn him, the view was just as good going as it had been coming.

Chapter 6

Laura took a deep, bracing inhale before knocking on the door to Carla and Jonah's new house. Although she barely got to see Carla before she'd become a globe-trotting television personality, she'd missed her cousin. They were only a few months apart in age, and Laura had spent virtually all her time with Carla before she'd joined the ballet school in favor of the Catholic school they'd attended together.

She expected to see baby Layla bouncing on her mother's hip when Carla opened the door. Instead, her cousin had both arms free to fling around Laura's neck.

"You're heeerreeee!"

Laura laughed at Carla's exuberance. Her cousin was the kind of person a lot of others underestimated. Her bubbly personality and the mostly one-sided conversations that meandered from Viking death rituals to the invite list at the Met Ball threw people off. But the people who stopped at the surface didn't know the real Carla Hernandez—Kane, now.

Laura reveled in her cousin—light to her dark, extrovert to her introvert. "Where's the baby?"

Carla pulled back and rolled her eyes. "You think I get to hold my own kid if Uncle Charlie's here?"

She was taken aback. Given all she knew about Charlie's checkered past, she wouldn't have taken him for a kid person. But his reluctance about giving her an annulment and walking out of her life quietly surprised her, too. With what she knew about his first marriage and how it had ended, she would have thought that he'd want to be rid of her and any potential for drama as quickly as possible.

"Are you sure you can trust him with her?"

Her cousin laughed and pulled her into the house, clinging to Laura's arm. "You obviously don't know him that well." She stopped and turned, grabbing both of her shoulders and giving her a very serious face that scared the shit out of Laura. It was a look that said she wasn't going to like the next thing that came out of her cousin's mouth. "I actually think you should get to know Charlie better. *Like a lot better.*"

All the blood rushed out of Laura's head, and she felt a little faint. She couldn't seem to make the words of denial come out of her mouth. Instead, she shook her head, which made her even more lightheaded.

"Now, just hear me out." She put the tip of her tongue in the corner of her lips. Before the wedding, Laura had observed Layla making a similar gesture. Right before she'd gone face first into a tower of cupcakes. "He's nothing like he was a decade ago."

Laura was starting to get that, but it didn't mean that she wanted to get romantically involved with Charlie. Not for real anyway. She had the feeling that a real relationship would put her at more risk than a sham marriage.

"I'm not looking for a relationship right now." She craned her neck, hoping that Carla's husband, Jonah, would interrupt them. "Can we go get a drink?"

"Since when are you a boozehound?"

"I'd like a glass of wine in my hand if you're going to throw me at a random guy." *A totally not random guy with a pretty face and pretty body and hands she was currently obsessed with.* "And I don't need you setting me up at all. I'm fine on my own."

Carla tugged her into the kitchen. "I just want you to be happy."

"And I'm happy." Not true. Or not entirely true. If she were happy, would she be clinging to the New York City Ballet so much? Wouldn't she laugh and smile with her partner instead of feel a knot in her stomach every time she went to rehearsal? A happy woman wouldn't hesitate to end her accidental marriage—she sure as hell wouldn't have signed annulment papers in her dresser. But she couldn't say any of that to her cousin. Not now that Carla finally had her happy. Laura turned and grabbed two glasses from the counter. "Red or white?"

"White." Carla opened the fridge and grabbed a bottle. "And I know that you've wanted to be a principal dancer since you were a little kid. But I also know *why* you want that, and you don't have to be worried that you'll turn into your mother."

Laura took a sip of the cold sauvignon blanc to collect her thoughts. Tears pricked the back of her eyes and she got angry at how well her cousin knew her. "I'm not going to give up my own life and trail all over the world for some guy."

Her cousin screwed up her face and stepped over to her. "Is that what you think I did?"

"No. I just—Jonah makes you happy. And that's great. You're equals." She looked down into the swirling liquid as though it would give her an answer. Needing words to describe why she and her cousin were so different. "Dancing is all I have. It's everything I know. *Some guy* is not going to replace that. I have to wait until dance is done with me and then figure out what I want to do with the rest of my life before I find someone."

Carla's shoulders relaxed. "But aren't you, maybe, done with ballet?"

"No." Not quite. Her stomach flipped even thinking about it. She took another sip. "I'm not done."

"You were so happy in Bali without rehearsals and stress and backstabbing. Don't you want that to be your life?"

"Life can't be a vacation." She sighed. "And even if I was done, I would have to figure something else out. I'm going to support myself. I can't rely on someone for my own security."

"But you can go on a few dates and have some fun, right?" Carla grabbed her free hand. "You're here tonight, and this is fun."

"Not right now it's not."

"Let's go find the boys. That'll be fun."

"For you, maybe."

"Just give Charlie a chance."

Laura was afraid that Charlie would run away with everything she had to give if she gave him even a little opening. He would take her time, her career, and very possibly her heart. She ached where that organ strained toward the fear. Only her brain and the logical reservations she had to getting even more involved with a man who—along with a few shots of tequila—had stolen her good sense once.

She steeled herself inside her mind as they walked out onto the lanai. Instead of giving in to the relaxing atmosphere and the good company, she prepared herself for battle.

* * * *

"Who's my best girl?" The baby smiled and showed her four teeth when Charlie made a funny face. Layla was maybe the best thing ever. It made him sick that he'd missed this with all of his nieces and nephews. He couldn't drop by his oldest brother's house and grill meat. He got pictures and homemade cards every so often, but they weren't personal.

He guessed it was weird that he'd grown attached to a kid that didn't belong to him. But on long trips around the world, Jonah and Carla had become like family. And the feelings now extended to their daughter.

It also helped that he was something of a baby whisperer. On a shoot in Rio, the nanny had gotten sick. They hadn't had money in the budget to extend the shoot, and the baby was too fussy for them to include her on the episode. Carla had been close to tears with frustration, and Charlie had made a face at the sobbing baby.

When she perked right up and laughed, they'd cemented their friendship, and the rest was history.

"I've got a front-runner right here." Carla's voice always had a winking quality to it. She was really amazing, and she made Jonah deliriously happy. Gorgeous and funny as hell. When he'd first met her in Havana, he'd decided that he was going to make a play for her if Jonah dropped the ball.

But when he turned and saw who she'd come out on the patio with, he couldn't even see Carla. When Laura came into a room he couldn't see another woman, couldn't recall how he'd ever found another woman attractive.

She wore a strappy sundress that she couldn't possibly have a bra on underneath. Her face, her long limbs, and the hint of a smile on her mouth. All of it together made her glow. She was his kryptonite, bracingly beautiful and twice as dangerous.

Probably not liking his attention off of her, Layla started to fuss. Jonah stepped away from the grill and grabbed his daughter. She planted her gummy smile into his shirt, likely leaving a trail of drool. For his part, Jonah rolled with it, offering up his tongs to his wife.

"Can you turn the steaks, princess?"

"I'm never going to get to hold my own kid, am I?"

"She likes me better than you." Jonah smiled more now that he was with Carla and had Layla in a way that made Charlie sick in a good way.

"That's one woman who likes you then." Both of them walked over to the grill, Jonah standing back to keep Layla out of the line of fire, literally.

That left Charlie to stare at his wife. She approached him tentatively.

"Apparently, this is a set-up." Her voice was quiet and she looked down.

He wanted to take the hair that had fallen in her face between his fingers and touch that silk. Tonight, she looked a lot like how she'd looked the night they'd met. Soft and ripe for picking. The fact that he couldn't touch her, couldn't kiss her without letting the cat out of the bag made him want to touch her all the more.

"Why are you just looking at me like that?" She sounded bewildered that he'd want to spend a whole lot of time looking at her. She could stop people's breath with a hand gesture, but she didn't realize what she did to him just by breathing.

"I like looking at you." Maybe more than he liked anything else.

"You're just full of lines, aren't you?"

"Be nice," Carla said over her shoulder from the grill. She'd reclaimed Layla from Jonah, but was lingering on the other side of the patio.

Charlie picked up his beer, just to keep from continuing to stare at Laura like a dolt. "It's not a line when it's true."

"Why am I supposed to believe anything that comes out of your mouth?"

"Have I ever lied to you?"

She doesn't even pause. "No." She looked chastened.

"I'm not going to start now." He took a step closer to her and she didn't move away. He caught a whiff of whatever soap or lotion she used—it was floral, like lilies or something else beautiful and rare. "I will never lie to you Laura, and I'll do whatever I have to do to convince you that I'm not the guy she said I was on that tape. She did lie about me, and I reacted badly." He paused to let it sink in with her that every damn thing his ex had said about him was a lie, especially the parts about him being bad in bed. "I'm older and wiser. And I know what I want."

"You don't want me."

"Wanna bet?"

This time, she stepped closer to him and whispered. "I maybe remember that it was a bet that got us into this."

"Yeah, you bet me that you could go shot for shot." Her outsized confidence had been hot. He liked that she'd sized him up and found him wanting. And that was the bitch about this whole thing. Maybe he only liked her because she didn't want him?

She took another sip of wine. "I'm not going to make that kind of bet tonight."

"Well, we can't get married twice, and we've already established that I don't take advantage of incapacitated women."

"We have." She inclined her head towards him, and something about the way her posture softened made him want to reach out and touch her even more.

"Can we just have a nice night with our friends?"

"I thought we already were."

He didn't struggle to find words very often. But he was at a loss. He wanted to show her nice, give her more nice. "I just—I want us to be friends."

"I have enough friends." She turned to him and squinted, as though everything he said aroused her suspicion. Not exactly the emotion he was aiming to arouse with her.

"We could all use more friends."

"I don't trust you."

That hit him in the chest and a ball of anger formed in his throat because he wanted her to trust him. Charlie looked over at Carla and Jonah, who seemed to be ignoring them but were probably just sneaky about watching them together.

"What would I have to do to earn your trust?" He ran his hand over his hair. "Carla and Jonah trust me with their kid, for Christ's sake."

"You're too much for me."

Funny, he thought it was the other way around.

Before he could ask any questions, dinner was ready. Reluctantly, he put his easygoing fun face back on for his friends, plotting to find out what Laura had meant later.

* * * *

Fuck Charlie Laughlin. Not literally, but figuratively and in a way he wouldn't enjoy. Tonight, he hadn't even done anything to piss her off that much. He just confused her, and surprised her. Laura didn't like being surprised by people. She liked to make her conclusions and put them in their respective boxes. She didn't like to fixate on people. Even when she was a kid her crushes had freaked her out. All that obsessive thinking had her wishing her life was different and those thoughts were dangerous.

It was the kind of thinking that had sent her mother straight to the bottom of a bottle of pills. A bottle she still lived in, to this day. Wishing destroyed lives.

And seeing Charlie with Layla hit her right in the ovaries. She'd always figured that children weren't going to happen for her. By the time she gave up professional dance, her reproductive organs would be calcified. And she'd been fine with that possibility. But seeing her husband—that word was coming too quickly to mind when she thought about him these days—with his thumb clutched in a chubby, baby hand had filled her with longing.

She sawed at her filet mignon with way too much intensity, making her plate skid across the table, narrowly missing her wineglass. Jonah and Carla looked at her quizzically, and Charlie smirked at her infuriatingly. That he knew he got under her skin got under her skin even more.

Just being here, being normal, made her want this more often. She wished she could have more than a glass-and-a-half of wine, wished she could stay out here listening to her cousin and her husband chat with Charlie until midnight. Instead, she was about to turn into a pumpkin at ten. If she didn't get at least nine hours of sleep tonight, she'd have yet another worthless rehearsal tomorrow.

And she could feel Matthieu getting more and more frustrated with her. If they weren't friends, then he already would have replaced her. Five years ago, that thought would have filled her with shame. Now, she struggled to care.

The only intense emotion that filled her was the waves of lust and something else she couldn't quite name coming off the man she remained temporarily married to. He didn't have to say anything, she just felt it. His sexual interest was overwhelming even without the occasional brush of his hand or their knees touching under the table.

She worked hard not to show that she was affected by him, to keep her body from drifting toward him.

When they were done eating the delicious steak and asparagus, Carla stood up. "Dessert?"

"None for me." The meal had already had too much oil for her diet. "I'll come in and help you serve, though."

"I'll eat her serving," Charlie said. He put the emphasis on the first three words of that sentence.

Carla brushed off her offer of help. "Jonah's going to help." Her cousin's wink didn't leave any doubt that the objective of fetching dessert was to give her and Charlie a few moments alone.

To his credit, Charlie waited until his friends were out of earshot before leaning over and saying, "You don't have to be so nervous."

His words frittered through her system like lightening, setting every nerve ending to attention. "You just insinuated that you want to eat me."

He chuckled. "I don't have to *insinuate* anything at all." Her heart nearly stopped when he tugged her chair over close to him. "I can't think about nearly anything else but getting my mouth on you."

"You're being crass." And she really liked it, not that she would say that out loud.

"You don't seem to be responding to me acting like a gentleman." He ran a finger over the exposed skin of her collarbone. It was such an intimate touch she ought to have pulled away, but he had her enthralled, waiting for the next thing to come out of his mouth, hoping it was filthy. "So, I think I need to change the game."

"Won't make a difference."

He leaned even closer and his breath warmed her skin and gave her a chill all at the same time. He'd had wine with dinner so she smelled that but also felt like she'd been doused with pheromones. Being this close to him made her feel like she was floating, and any second he'd disappear and she'd crash to the ground.

"Of course it will make a difference. Do you think I don't know why your legs are rubbing together? Your body wants my cock right there." She hadn't even noticed she was squirming in her chair. Then, he reached his hand under the armrest and cupped her over her dress. She ought to move his hand, maybe bend his arm back so hard that it broke. He shouldn't be touching her, and she shouldn't like it. She shouldn't want more.

But—God help her—she did.

"I think you want, no need, to lose control." That was the last thing she needed, but she said nothing and willed him to say more. "Give me one night. Both of us sober." He squeezed, and she gripped the armrests of her chair until her knuckles ached. "And I'll show you how good it can be."

She felt like a shaken-up bottle of champagne, not caring that her cousin and Jonah were bound to walk out on them while Charlie was fondling her. Handling her. Nearly making her come.

All that wanting for something different converged on wanting Charlie. If they could actually leave it at one night, maybe she would get out unscathed. Maybe he would leave her alone. Even addled by being on the edge of coming, she knew it wasn't likely. Their chemistry was like a heavy blanket. It was nothing like she'd ever experienced before, but she knew it wouldn't be over in one go.

"One night?"

When she looked at him, he looked totally different to her than he ever had before. His brow was furrowed, his gaze serious. Some tender thing inside her wanted to smooth out the lines on his face; she wanted to soothe him. She knew one way to do that, and it couldn't possibly slake her thirst for him.

Just one night.

"If that's all you'll give me, I'll take it." He moved his hand down her thigh, and she wanted to protest, but she heard steps on the patio. His fingers on the skin of her thigh when he got past the hem of her dress made her jump. "But I'm not going to say that I don't want more."

He brushed his lips against her cheek as he backed off. She didn't miss the looks from both Jonah and Carla—him warning and her giddy—when they walked out and found her and Charlie closer.

Chapter 7

After dinner, she'd followed him in her car to his place. The whole ride over, it was as though something had taken over her body. Her brain kept telling her to get on the freeway and head towards downtown, but her body wouldn't listen.

"This is your house?" Laura looked around the open floor plan. From the front door, the sight line to the canal was clear. Everything was white—fabric, marble, and glass. The pink light from the setting sun touched every surface, but it didn't make the house look feminine.

"No, I'm taking you to someone else's house to have my wicked way with you." He surprised her by kissing the back of her neck and moving her with his tall frame over to the living room. Even being used to someone picking her up, a curl of pleasure worked through her at the way he moved her body. He didn't ask, he just took. That's not a quality she'd ever liked or looked for in a lover. The only thing she'd wanted or expected from sex in the past was a temporary physical release. Something like a massage or a satisfyingly difficult rehearsal.

This was bigger, not just because of the fact that Charlie had inserted himself into her career. If things went badly and he opened up his mouth, there would be hell to pay. No. He wouldn't do that. Despite telling him that she didn't trust him, something about Charlie felt safe. As safe as taking a flying leap off a cliff could be.

The frisson of anxiety buzzing through her brain was about how he made her body feel, simply by touching her casually, as though he had the right to.

He edged her over to the back of the couch and stepped back. One hand he kept curled around the back of her neck, keeping her still. She'd worn the backless dress to drive him crazy. The way he looked at her made her think he was imagining himself running his tongue all over her skin.

"I like it." She didn't know whether she was referring to the house or to the way he was touching her, the way she could feel his gaze all over her bared skin. Probably the latter.

"I like it, too." He leaned close, so his hot breath touched her neck and ear. "I wouldn't have bought it if I didn't like it."

"I'm not doing this because you sponsored the ballet."

His fingers tightened against her neck at her statement. "I didn't think you were." He paused, and ran his thumb over a knot at the side of her neck. "Has anyone ever thought that you were for sale like that?"

She shouldn't be honest with him. It really wasn't any of his business, and it might interfere with the heavenly way his hands were making her feel. But she couldn't help it. His charisma was so powerful to her that he didn't even have to prompt her openness, her honesty. "Most of those guys realize quick that they're barking up the wrong tree with me. I'm not for sale. Especially since most of those guys are married."

"Yeah, it's complicated when they're married to someone else." He stepped close again, and the heat of his body made her knees turn to Jell-O. "But, for the moment, you're married to me."

"Just a few more days." *She hoped.* If she could get herself to file the papers. And, if tonight worked in getting him out of her system, she could do it tomorrow.

"Doesn't change the fact that I wouldn't have married you if I hadn't wanted to do this." He brushed his lips against the skin at the crux of her shoulder and neck. She gasped and leaned back into him.

He moved his hands down to the hem of her dress, and he didn't stop kissing her neck while he edged the garment up with his fingertips. The room was dark and no one would see them, even if their boat was fairly close to the dock. But that didn't stop her from feeling exposed and vulnerable from his touch.

Fire erupted her skin everywhere he touched her, but he held her still when she tried to turn and kiss him. She still hadn't kissed him on the mouth without the haze of Mai Tais in the way. His lush and talented mouth moved down her spine, gradually, terribly slowly.

"Your back is beautiful. So strong."

"What are you doing?"

"Kissing you."

She groaned in frustration when he reached her lower back and painted her lower spine with his tongue.

He chuckled. "You're only going to give me one night, and I can't even take my time?"

"No." She tried to sound stern, but his hands were under her dress, and he was playing with her lace underwear. Her hope that he would get down to business, with his hands, his mouth, the cock she knew was ready for her kept her from saying something snarky.

"News flash, gorgeous." He pushed her mid back until she leaned over the back of the couch, and her ass was right in his face. "I'm not going to fuck you until you really need it. And I just don't believe you want it that badly right now."

She gritted her teeth to keep from begging him to just fuck her already. When he flipped her skirt up and pulled her panties down, she squealed. He laughed again, a dark, rich sound that didn't do anything good for her piece of mind.

He ran one finger down the center of her back and her over the crack of her ass. It was so filthy that she was sure her cheeks—both sets—were flushed. "What are you doing?"

"Be quiet."

"Don't tell me what to do."

"You'll do what I say if you want my mouth on you."

The way his breath felt against her core made her knees weak. She was all too ready to beg for him to do something to her. Anything but looking at her in a frankly lewd position.

When he ran his fingers up her inner thighs, she realized that she'd been quiet, so he was going to make her come. He stopped caressing when he got to the seam between her thigh and the core of her. It felt as though her skin rippled up from the shock of his touch. She wanted more, needed more.

Instead of being embarrassed, she was shoving her crotch in his face. He brought out something feral in her, and it should terrify her. But it didn't right then. She wanted to fall into him and forget everything outside of these four walls.

Just for one night.

"Up on your toes." For a few breaths, she didn't respond to his command. When he pinched the back of her thigh, the sharp pain made her reach up on her toes. "Good girl."

"I'm not a—" Her comeback got cut off when he licked her center.

"Fuck you taste good." He said the words right into her pussy, and they vibrated through her entire body. He worked her up so fast, she had to grip the upholstery on the couch so she wouldn't fall over. Her muscles strained, and her bones felt as though they could crack from the delicious, tight, excruciating sensations he pulled from her body.

"Oh, fuck. Like that." She was shameless in seeking out the orgasm he was trying to pull from her almost violently.

Right before she broke apart, he stopped. He pulled back and replaced his mouth with his fingers. When she let out a lazy whine, he smacked her ass with the hand that wasn't keeping her on the edge of a colossal, cataclysmic orgasm. He didn't move that hand away. Instead, he gripped her flesh and opened her up further.

It was filthy and made her so conscious of how everything was just right there in his face. "If I let you come, are you going to walk out?"

His voice sounded unsure, and that surprised her. Even after their not-great first date, he hadn't seemed to lose any of that maddeningly attractive cocksureness. Hearing him sound like he wasn't absolutely certain he had control over every bit of what was going on assuaged some of the self-consciousness of being bent over the couch with his face in her ass.

"I'll walk out right now if you don't make me come."

Instead of doing what he was told, he stood up, and pulled her up to standing. Her bare ass brushed the front of his pants. Still on her toes, she could feel his hard cock through only a thin layer of fabric. With a man as finely built as this, who had her on the edge of destruction by pleasure, she couldn't help but sway against him.

He grunted when her body disrupted the sensitive positioning of his erection, and some weird form of feminine satisfaction floated through her. It disappeared when he pulled down the straps of her dress so roughly that she feared they might rip. Going home topless was not on the agenda.

She bit her tongue when he took her nipples between fingers of each hand and rolled them almost roughly. His mouth went back to her neck, lips still damp from her core, making her feel all the more vulnerable and open to him.

The sky had darkened completely, and the only light in the room was from a single overhead above the sink. There was only enough light for her to see them there. His dark head bent over her shoulder, his fingers plumping up and torturing her nipples until she writhed against him. He grunted again, so she rolled her body again. His grip got tighter, and she moaned.

"What are you doing to me?"

"I'd say that you're the one doing all the doing."

"No. You're rolling that tease of a body against me again, torturing my cock every time you twitch that perfect ass." As if to demonstrate, he lowered one hand to her pussy and the other he held around her neck loosely.

When his fingers reached her clit, her whole body jumped. Unbelievably, she was even more primed than before. He could control her body so easily. When he held her like this, he could take whatever he wanted from her, and she would gladly give it to him.

Maybe it was that thought that finally broke her. Coming without him inside her was almost painful. Pleasure buzzed through her whole system, but she'd wanted his cock. After all it was so close, rubbing against her but not giving her what she needed from him.

"Fuck, fuck, fuck. Please."

She couldn't see the expression on his face in the reflection from the window, but she could only hope that he was as close to wrecked as she was.

* * * *

Charlie liked making Laura come. Actually, "like" wasn't the right word. He liked cold beer on a hot day. He craved the feel of Laura's body coming apart in his arms like he wanted water after a heavy night of drinking. He felt like he'd die without having it again and again and again.

Even though his cock demanded to be part of the next again, he stood there holding her, making soothing sounds until she settled against him, almost boneless. To know that he'd done that to her—for her—made him feel like nothing else.

Nothing in his professional life, nothing he'd ever seen travelling around the world would ever compare to having Laura claw his forearm, pushing him to give her more and somehow pulling away at the same time.

He'd pulled the pleasure out of her like a long-held secret. She was an anathema to him in a lot of ways, but every mysterious facet made him want to know more about her. After their fight at the ballet studio, he'd looked up videos of her dancing. It was hard to believe that someone as strong and as solid as Laura could make her movements look weightless. She wasn't bigger than other ballerinas, but seeing all that power up close made him think of her other contradictions.

That first dinner, she'd looked down her nose at him. But holding her in his arms tonight, bending her over the back of his couch as though he had some sort of claim on her, making her writhe uncontrollably at the height of her pleasure made him see that she was dark and light and all extreme measures.

Now that she was laid out on his bed, almost naked—just her dress twisted and hopelessly wrinkled around her waist. Her eyes almost black;

her gaze was glassy and unfocused. That wouldn't do because he wanted her right here with him.

He grimaced and she smiled at him lazily. He loved the way she looked completely undone. Her black hair a stark contrast against his white linens, messy. He crawled up on the bed and knelt up, looming over her, memorizing how she looked like this for him. "I like your hair like that."

"Messy?" She drew her big toe up his thigh. He caught her foot by the arch before she nudged his cock. It would be embarrassing if she tried and likely succeeded to get him off with a foot job. He was kind of a kinky bastard—after all he'd eaten her out from behind tonight and he hadn't even kissed her on the mouth yet. But foot fetishist he was not.

"Watch it, gorgeous."

"Watch it?" Her smile got bigger and made even more blood rush to his cock. "I haven't even seen it yet."

"You've felt it though." He rubbed himself over his pants, but it didn't relieve the almost unbearable ache of not being inside of her right now. "And you've tortured it."

"You call a few bumps and grinds torture?"

"You've been torturing it ever since Bali."

"That's your own damned fault, though." She wrenched her foot free from his hand and ran her shin between his legs. "I'm fairly sure I offered to take care of it."

He caught her foot again, and pulled the dress from her waist. Naked Laura was the best Laura, and he had to take a moment to appreciate her grandeur. "You were drunk, and that wouldn't have been right."

"You're such a gentleman."

"I'm surprised to hear that after what just happened in the living room."

"I think it's downright chivalrous that you made me come first."

"You think that was me being considerate?" She nodded, and he came over her on all fours. "No, gorgeous, that was pure selfishness. I *wanted* to taste you there so bad that I don't even remember what we had for dinner tonight." He palmed her between her thighs, satisfied that his hand came away wet. He pumped one finger into her and shifted his other hand to her clavicle, feeling her pulse speed up and her skin heat. "I needed to know that you would give over to me more than I want to fuck you right now."

Her eyes dipped to his lap. "You want to fuck me a whole lot?" Her voice was breathy, and she was close again. He could feel it. She turned him into a predator, and it filled him with something he didn't recognize. He'd never felt like he wanted to conquer a woman before. And he'd never felt this needy kind of pulling in his gut to take and dominate. It disturbed him a little, but that faded away when he realized how much it turned her on for him to take control.

"I want to fuck you so much that I'm afraid it will fall off if I don't get inside you soon."

"That's not a thing." She snaked one of her hands between his legs and undid his belt and his pants. He knelt up and pulled off his shirt. Instead of moving closer to the goal of putting him out of his misery, she trailed her hand over his stomach. He was glad he was up to her standards. When he'd seen the guy she danced with every day—how close and intimate that was—he felt like maybe he wouldn't measure up. He'd always been tall and lean, had a hard time putting on muscle, but he wasn't used to feeling like he might not be enough.

The way she was looking at him made him feel like he was the only thing she wanted, and he couldn't help but lean over and kiss her. She moaned and opened to him, gave him so much in her kiss. She didn't stop kissing him, but she pulled up her legs around his waist and pushed his pants the rest of the way down with her toes. Her high arches against his thighs were going to make him rethink the whole foot fetish thing.

He was so close to being inside her that his cock bumped against her inner thigh. They must have been thinking the same thing when he pulled back to grab protection from the side drawer.

"Condom?" she said. Her lips were swollen and almost magenta.

He rifled around in the drawer and pulled one out. "Always."

He got the condom on faster than anyone had ever put a condom on before. "Ready?"

"I wouldn't still be naked if I wasn't."

He smiled into her neck, kissed the soft skin there and sank into her. Right at that moment, the air changed around them. He became aware of nothing other than the sensation of touching her, of feeling her body against his, the smell of her mixed with him.

Jesus, she was something else. Every time he withdrew she followed him, giving everything to him right back. Her arms wrapped around him, keeping him close, filling his chest with a sensation he couldn't name.

He moved at a steady pace until her mouth found his earlobe and she bit down. The tiny shock of pain spurred him on and she moaned with satisfaction.

"You're a little hell cat, aren't you?" He didn't expect an answer, so he kept talking. "You keep everything all buttoned up and tight with bobby pins, cover up this body with sequins and feathers." He slipped a hand down to where their bodies met and rubbed. Her eyes flew open, and she met his gaze. "That's right. Look at me when I'm telling you that whole 'ice queen' thing is a front. You have so much fucking passion, and you only give it to me."

Her eyes widened in shock before she went to close them. He couldn't let her do that. He needed her right there with him for this. If he was going to convince her that they should be together, he had to keep her with him as she was now—wild. If he let her forget how they made each other feel, then she would retreat. The next time he saw her, she'd pretend she didn't know him. At least not like this. She'd treat him like a stranger, and the idea of that made him see spots in his peripheral vision.

"If you can't look in my face while I'm fucking you, I can take you from behind." He stroked the column of her throat with his thumb. "Is that what you want?" She nodded, so he withdrew, flipped her over, and put her on her knees. "I don't mind looking at this glorious ass and your back arched for my cock." He reentered her, and her body curved up.

She backed up into him until he was inside her to the hilt. From this angle, he was deeper, so deep she whimpered. "Am I hurting you?" She shook her head and followed him when he tried to move away, just a little, whimpering. He threaded his fingers through the hair at the back of her scalp, not pulling. "I'm not going to hurt you, but I'm going to hold you while I fuck you."

"Yes." Her words were a throaty gasp.

Something about making this woman feel so much that she could hardly speak made him wild and he pumped into her so hard the bed frame moved across the floor. He was going to come soon, but she needed to come while he was inside her. "Rub your clit, Laura. I need to feel you coming around my cock before I let go." She shook her head again, and he stilled her. "You want me to stop?"

"N—no. Don't stop."

"Then rub your clit, gorgeous." He grabbed one ass cheek and rubbed one of his fingers over her asshole. She jumped and moved one of her hands between her legs. Almost immediately, her inner muscles started flexing around him. He gritted his teeth to keep from orgasming inside her right then. "Are you close?"

"Yes. So close."

"What do you need?"

"H-harder." He'd bet he was the only man who'd ever made her stammer and beg for it harder. One look down her nose and most would scurry away. Maybe it was because he was her husband—for about another minute—that he felt like he wanted to tear down the wall she had up in between her and everything sensual and earthy and uncontrolled. Perhaps it was just the way their two chemistries meshed. He didn't know, but he would give her whatever she asked for in that soft raspy voice.

"I'll give you whatever you want Laura, whatever I have." The next day she'd forget he said that, and pretend that this was simply fucking. But he had to tell her how he really felt when he was this wide open to her, when she'd stripped off the civilized man parts of him to reveal a Neanderthal who just needed to claim, and fuck, and mark.

When she came, the arm holding her up collapsed. Between that and her pussy squeezing him, he was toast, done. His brain couldn't work and roll over. He didn't even have the brain power to think about making sure she didn't leave in the middle of the night.

He didn't black out, but he definitely came back to himself in stages. No memory of collapsing on top of her spent body while still inside her. It took him a few moments to be able to move again. He pulled out of her, and his muscles protested. Before going into the bathroom to get cleaned up and get rid of the condom, he kissed the back of her neck. She stirred, and the fear that she would leave came right back.

"Don't move."

"I don't think I could if I tried." He could see her smiling through the strands of hair that lay across her face.

"Did I break you?" He chuckled. "If I did, does that mean I get to keep you?"

When her smile faded, he walked into the *en suite*, moving faster because he was afraid she'd slip through his fingers.

When he returned, she was still in the same spot, and relief flashed through him like a summer storm. He stretched out next to her on the bed, placing his hand on her back as though it would hold her here. Her eyes were drooping, almost closed. Having her here and getting to see her mussed up and sleepy—satisfied—fulfilled the part of himself that she'd revealed.

He realized that he'd been a little bit asleep before. Although he'd moved to Miami to get away from the expectation that he would be the same heartless captain of industry his father was, he'd lost touch with having any real ambition at all. And, being with Laura made him realize that he had ambition, but maybe it was different than his father's had been. She made him want to protect her, build a future with her.

The sad irony of it all was that a future with him would cost her everything she wanted.

Chapter 8

Sneaking into her own home the night after a one-night stand was not something Laura had ever envisioned herself doing. She hadn't done it as a teenager. And, as an adult, she'd never had the need.

She turned the lock in the door quietly, opened the door slowly so it wouldn't creak. Held her shoes in her hand so they wouldn't clack all over the hardwoods.

But she needn't have bothered. By the time she got to the credenza where she stored her bag, she realized that her grandmother, the person she was trying to sneak in to avoid, was on the couch.

And she wasn't alone.

Mortification gummed up the blood in Laura's veins and she stood stock still as she took in what was happening. Grandma Lola was making out with someone who looked very much like Laura's grandfather. Laura had never seen her grandparents kiss; she hadn't seen them together until Carla's wedding. And they hadn't spoken at that event, much less groped each other.

She wasn't a preteen, and she knew older people got frisky, but this was a shock on so many levels. Her grandparents had been divorced for almost thirty-five years. As soon as her grandfather decided to flee Cuba, he'd become a stranger to her grandmother. According to the family lore, she'd chased him out of her family home with a knife, screaming that he was a traitor. She would have gotten him killed by the government if anyone had been of the mind to snitch.

Even when he'd bribed enough people to take her with him and their nearly grown children, she'd refused to leave. Refused to give up her home.

No one in the family understood that decision to this day. Her mother barely spoke to Lola when she came to the house. Laura's aunt refused to see her.

Lola had remained close with her nephew, Hector, through letters. Laura had never gotten the full story on why that happened. Why her grandmother had refused to leave and given up her children.

And now, she was watching her grandparents make out. If she'd had any breakfast, it would have come up. Had Lola been sneaking around with her ex-husband? Is that why she wouldn't say where she'd been the other night?

Ew. Gross. Gag. They all came to mind. Watching her grandparents roll around on her sectional was like watching a flamingo try to mate with a shark. Someone was going to get dead and bloody if she didn't put a stop to this.

Laura cleared her throat, and her *abuelo*'s head popped up.

"You weren't supposed to be home." With more grace than she should have at her age, Lola extricated herself from the clinch and wiped errant lipstick from the side of her mouth, looking none too guilty.

"What's—what's going on here?"

Lola tilted her head as if to convey, "Oh dear, am I going to have to give her 'the talk'?"

In order to avoid that, Laura started towards the hall leading to the bedrooms. Before she got three steps, her grandfather said, "This is not what it looks like."

Laura turned slowly, and took in her grandfather's half-buttoned shirt and her grandmother's mussed up hair. She pursed her lips and nodded. "So, I didn't walk in on my long-divorced grandparents sucking each other's faces off?"

Neither of them had anything to say to that. They just sat on the couch, looking like teenagers who were caught necking.

"I need to shower and get to rehearsal." Laura looked to her grandmother. "I think we should have dinner together tonight. Get some wine. I'm going to need it to hear you explain this."

Laura waved her shoes between the two of them, and they had the courtesy to look sheepish. They, of course, had the right to do whatever they wanted. They were adults, both in full command of their faculties. But she felt like she had the right to maybe not *see* it?

When she got to her room and stripped off her clothes, she was reminded of places on her body raw and tender from what she and Charlie had consented to as adults the night before. When she got in the shower, she couldn't help but run her fingers over the places where his beard had scraped her skin, places she wouldn't expect like all over her thighs, her lower back. He'd been so different last night—not at all what she'd expected.

Before they'd fucked she'd thought he was this laid-back guy sort of floating by on his dad's money and connections. The show he produced for Jonah and Carla was good, but the stuff he'd done before in Chicago had been reality dating shows that pitted women with low self-esteem against each other to compete for a douchey, vacant dude bro. Those kinds of shows made Laura a little sick inside.

But last night, his touch had revealed a different side of him. There'd been nothing laid back about the way he took her, talked to her, commanded her body with his. Before he'd done dirty, filthy things to her, she'd enjoyed looking at him. Now, she couldn't get the sound of his voice out of her head. She'd agreed to spend one night with him, but she wouldn't be able to keep her fingers from creeping into her panties when she was alone. Wouldn't be able to stop the slow burn of the fire he'd lit inside her the night before from taking over. For the next long while, whenever she made herself come, she'd only be able to think about him and how well he'd learned her body in a few short hours.

She almost wished that she hadn't limited their affair to one night. Although she'd never admit that she wanted more, her curiosity about Charlie had been piqued. It was the same curiosity that had gotten her to take her first ballet class at three after seeing a poster for the Miami City Ballet. Standing in her bathroom now, facing the likelihood that she'd never get to be with Charlie again, she wasn't sure that she was living her life right. Something in her gut burned with regret—the idea of those papers she had to file so she could get where she wanted to be in life.

She shook her head, wincing when a drop of shampoo got in her eye. She didn't have time to think about what might have been if she hadn't lost all control for one night with Charlie Laughlin. What was done was done, and other than opening night, she'd probably never have to see him again.

* * * *

Charlie sat in the darkened theater, not wanting her to see him watching them block portions of the ballet. He felt like a creeper, and he should be at work. But after spending a long night in bed with the star of the show and waking up just in time for her to leave him hard and wanting this morning, his dick was fully in charge of his schedule. That was the only explanation for the fit of madness that brought him here.

At first, he'd only sponsored the ballet so he could see her again. It was an extremely expensive way to make sure she got that second date, but totally worth it. He would have paid more because he was a sucker for the way Laura moved. But watching her sweat-covered and straining today was markedly different than feeling her come apart in his arms the night before. Gone was the passionate, wanton woman from last night. Even from a hundred feet away, he could see the lines of strain on her face and the difficulty she was having performing each step. She was still almost perfect, and he probably wouldn't have noticed the looks on her face unless he'd seen her the way she was last night. But now that he'd seen her face lax with bliss, he knew—knew—that she was not blissful while dancing. At least not anymore.

He wondered if it was just being tired of dancing in Miami. Although this was a very different production of *Carmen*—performed with opera singers doing vocals live on the edge of the stage and brand new choreography—she'd performed this piece in different incarnations ten times. Or so he'd memorized from what he could find online. Because he'd done research on his erstwhile wife. *Like a creeper.*

When the choreographer cued the dancers to begin the opening sequence again, someone slid into the seat behind him. Assuming that it was another dancer or someone associated with the company, Charlie didn't look over his shoulder until the person tapped his shoulder.

"Charlie Laughlin, right?"

Then he turned and saw a guy who didn't seem to be associated with the ballet. He was, however, holding a pad and pen. Having grown up around a lot of his father's subordinates, there were several signs that this was a reporter.

"And you are?"

"Phil Oliveras, *Ocean Drive.*"

Charlie raised his brow. "And my identity matters to you, how?"

"I'm doing a story on your wife, so I'd think my identity matters to you plenty."

The bottom dropped out of Charlie's stomach. He hadn't told anyone anything about his sham marriage. And the way Laura had threatened to gut him if he told anyone told him that she had kept her mouth shut, too. His mind ran through the possibilities—her family or the waiter.

He imagined that her grandparents would have kept the confidence. The waiter, however, had no reason not to talk. The murderous looks Charlie had dealt him during dinner might have provided motivation.

Still, he schooled his features and didn't respond to the reporter. If he had anything solid, there would have been a blind item out on their marriage at the very least. Since he was still at the goading and making annoying innuendo phase, he didn't have anything to go on. Although a trip to the clerk's office might remedy that if the annulment papers hadn't gone through yet.

Fuck.

"Wife?"

"You're married to Laura Delgado."

Charlie shrugged. "That's really breaking news when the groom doesn't even know."

The reporter rolled his eyes behind his trendy horn-rimmed glasses. "Drop the shit, Laughlin. You know how this game is played. Hell, you've staged multiple versions of the game, televised all over the world. Just give me a quote."

Anger balled Charlie's fists. Only the fact that he didn't want to disrupt Laura's rehearsal or get arrested for turning this guy's facial features into something that resembled ground beef kept him from clocking him, repeatedly. And the reporter was just doing his job. The fact that he'd gone out with his wife, kissed her in public before the annulment went through put them at risk for publicity.

He hated the fact that he'd ever signed on to produce that dating show after his first marriage had ended in a hail of gossip gunfire. But he'd been young and it had been fun. He'd reveled in the attention he got for it. Every news story about how the show was in poor taste—especially the ones that had embarrassed his father—had delighted him. But now? At this moment, he was wondering if he could take on a new identity because his current one had been an unredeemable asshole—totally erase the reason Laura didn't see him as a real possibility for herself.

"What would it take for you to just cover the ballet and not mention any relationship between me and Ms. Delgado?"

"Are you trying to bribe me?"

"No. I never mentioned money." Charlie had chosen his gambit carefully. But he had something else that might be of interest to his new buddy, Phil. Access.

"But you implied—"

Charlie turned away from the reporter, and said, "Fuck what I implied. What do you want?"

"Besides photos of the happy couple?" The sarcasm in this motherfucker's voice coated the air and made Charlie sick to his stomach. "I want the whole story—how you two met, the engagement story, and the wedding night."

If he'd looked back at Phil in that moment, he was pretty sure his looks would kill the guy dead. As tempting as that was, it was more important that he extricate himself—and more importantly Laura—from this situation without bloodshed.

"You're not getting any of that because none of it exists."

"Why don't you look me in the face and tell me that?"

"Do you like your job?"

Phil barked out a laugh that got the dancers' and choreographer's attention. *Just fucking great.*

"This is a closed rehearsal." The choreographer's voice was faint but emphatic.

Not wanting to be found out for creeping on Laura, Charlie got up wordlessly and walked out of the theater. Reluctantly, he motioned for the scumbag reporter to follow him. Once they were out in the lobby, Charlie faced the guy, folding his arms so he wouldn't clock him.

"Again, Phil, do you like your job?"

"I went to Columbia J school, and I write puff pieces for a local magazine. Does that seem like a job that someone like me would like?"

Charlie looked the guy up and down. From the lack of care towards his appearance, he subscribed to the school of thought that real journalists looked like schlubs at all times. "So, what do you want to let this go?"

"Listen, buddy—"

"I'm not your fucking buddy." Charlie leaned down and got in Phil's face. He softened his voice. "I'm not going to be your buddy or help you get out of a job you hate if you don't play ball."

"I have integrity." When Charlie didn't respond, just tilted his head, he continued. "I do—and the way you're trying not to hit me right now tells me I'm right."

"What would it matter if you were?" Sure, Laura was a local celebrity, and her extended family was a regular item on local gossip blogs, but that didn't mean that her getting married warranted whatever kind of serious investigative journalism that this guy thought he was doing. "Neither of us are famous." And Charlie had worked hard to stop being infamous for the past few years. "Why are you wasting your time?"

"You think it's not big news that the original producer of the *The Single Guy*, the guy who said all those things about his ex-wife and the women on your show, got married to a classy, fine-assed prima ballerina." Charlie fingers twitched with the need to twist Phil's outer ear right off his head. Laura was *his* fine-assed ballerina. At least for the time being. "That's news in this little corner of the world."

"And not even a byline on a national newspaper would talk you out of it?"

"If I break this story, I can get the same thing on any arts page I want."

"Not on any of the papers my father owns."

"Really? Last I heard, the two of you weren't speaking. He'd really carry out a vendetta for you?"

"It's not a vendetta. I just don't think that a gutter-dwelling loser belongs on any of my dad's papers." He was vastly exaggerating his influence with dear-old-dad, but one of his brothers would do him a solid for sure. "I've got to protect the family name."

Really, the only name he wanted to protect was Laura's. She didn't deserve to be linked with him in perpetuity. She deserved to get everything she wanted—even if what she wanted was in New York and thousands of miles away from him. But telling fuckhead Phil that wasn't going to help his case.

"I don't think you have that much influence anymore."

Charlie got so far in Phil's face that the other guy had to back up. "Watch me." Phil turned white as a sheet. "Get out of here before she sees you. You breathe wrong in her direction a decade from now, and I will end you. Not just your career. You. You are full of shit, and your story means nothing. But I like Laura and her family. You cause her one iota of pain and you'll be shitting from a tube."

As soon as he said the words, he knew it was too much. When the door to the theater slammed and Phil looked over his shoulder with pancake-sized eyes, Charlie knew someone had heard his declaration of war in favor of Laura. Anyone hearing that would know that Laura meant something to him, exactly the opposite of what he should have conveyed to the jackass in front of him.

And it was even worse because it was her.

Charlie didn't look back to see if Laura was standing there. He didn't have to. Her smell was unmistakable, and it wafted all the way over to where he was standing. Her standing in a room wasn't something he could ignore. She was undeniable. Denying that they were married to the press was one thing. Denying that he was starting to have very real feelings for the gorgeous, intoxicating woman he was married to was very much another.

Sleeping with—claiming—Laura had been a huge mistake. Now, he would never get her out of his system. He'd never be able to forget the things that she'd given only to him. He didn't want to think about her career ending because of salacious gossip and fallout within the company. But he couldn't be distant or impartial with her. He had this insane need to protect her, even if it killed him to deny their connection to anyone.

He was afraid all of that hung in the vestibule, and that what he'd said to Phil would blow up for him—but mostly for Laura. All he wanted was to be alone with her so he could explain.

"Are you going to get the fuck out? Or do I have to call security?"

Chapter 9

"Honey." Laura approached Charlie and grabbed onto his arm, partially to keep him from grabbing the arts reporter from *Ocean Drive* by the throat and shaking him, and partially because she needed to as part of her new publicity plan with respect to her husband. Granted, it was a hastily assembled plan that she'd thought up while standing at the door to the theater just now, but it had to work. "There's no need to talk to Phil that way."

The flex and pull in Charlie's biceps muscles told her that he very much felt the need to come through on the threats he'd just lobbed. "There isn't?" She swore that the sound of Charlie's back teeth grinding filled the space. And damn her, it was so hot to hear him talk that way.

"No, because we're going to cooperate in the story." Her husband's body tensed up, and doubt crept in about whether or not she'd done the right thing. After all, she didn't know him that well. She knew the parts that lingered online from a decade ago, but he'd stayed mostly out of the public eye since then.

She was getting to know the man he was now, and he was much more private than he had been in his twenties. Seeing him with baby Layla, having a relaxed dinner with friends, going home with him afterwards—all of that was giving her a very different picture of Charlie Laughlin.

Letting him beat the crap out of an annoying and slimy reporter wasn't what he wanted. She didn't think. The way he'd defended her had given her a thrill that she didn't want to examine too closely. Seeing him here, knowing that he'd been watching her made her feel things that she didn't know how to place.

Charlie's presence was confusing, but it felt right in this elemental way. It made her want to protect him the only way she knew how.

Maybe people knowing about them wasn't the worst thing in the world. She wasn't ready to share all the gory, drunken details about how they'd gotten together, but a whirlwind romance might not completely tank her career. It might even get asses in seats to the opening show of the season, which was only a few weeks away.

"Yes." She clasped Charlie's hand, and he looked down at her with surprise marking his features. She smiled up at him, as adoringly as she could muster. The sex must have addled her brain or something because it was easy to look up at him as though she was in love with him. Lust was a powerful drug.

"My cousin, Carla Hernandez, introduced us. We were both part of the wedding party, and spent a lot of time together for that. Love was just in the air, so we decided to take the plunge."

Phil finally found the balls to open his mouth, probably easier since Charlie's posture had eased slightly and Laura managed to pull him back and occupy one of his hands. "So, it's true? You actually got married?"

"Yes. We're married." Charlie's smile bit through the rest of her fear and resistance. The satisfaction of making him happy frightened her.

"In Bali."

"At your cousin's wedding? Didn't that steal focus from the bride?"

Laura looked up at Charlie. He winked at her, and heat spilled through her system. The silent communication between them was new to her. She had glimpses of it with some of her frequent dance partners, but it was novel with a romantic partner. And Charlie was now more than her fake husband. He was her real husband, and her real lover.

"We did it privately, and we hadn't wanted to tell anyone else for a while." He squeezed her hand, and she had to look down at the floor to keep herself from beaming at him. All this warmth and affection she was getting from him felt embarrassing. She usually ran away from men who treated her like they really wanted her because they always wanted too much.

And Charlie's intensity last night made her feel something similar, but different. It was new and exciting because she wanted him back and felt like she had something to offer him in return for the attention. He didn't feel like an inconvenience.

"And we'd like to keep most of it private." His words surprised her. Here she was opening herself to criticism and speculation, and he didn't want to subject her to that.

"But, freedom of the press—"

"You really think that two people who are sort of in the public eye is on par with political scandal or intrigue?" Charlie's smooth, charming veneer was back.

"I think it's what I'm going to report on." The reporter shrugged. "Whether you cooperate or not."

Laura did not want this story reported on in a way that was scandalous. Undoubtedly, it would be worse for everyone involved. If they cooperated, she could buy time to warm up her parents to the idea that they were married. Charlie could tell his parents—if he wanted, which wasn't likely, but maybe. Either that, or hos mother would burn St. Patrick's down with candles.

If they really went public, and didn't treat this like it was an inconvenient rumor, they would have to stay married for a while. They could go live separately, but show up at events once in a while. And, in a year or two, they could get a quiet divorce.

"When do you want to set up a photo shoot?"

* * * *

Charlie was stunned at Laura's reaction to the reporter. He'd been sure she was going to fly off the handle and deny everything. He didn't have words for how amazing it felt to have her at his back.

And he barely waited until they got back in her dressing room after Oliveras-the-scumbag left before pressing her against the wall and covering her mouth with his. He didn't care that she was sweaty or that he wasn't supposed to be there. He just wanted her. Now.

The kiss was slow and grinding, laced with unmistakable intent. It was a promise of all the things he planning on doing to her now that they were publically married. He was going to get to touch her in public now. He wouldn't have to feel like a creepy stalker if he showed up to see his wife. *His wife.*

"You didn't have to do that." When he came up for air, he wanted to be sure that she was really okay with going public. That she didn't feel like she'd been pushed into a corner. He needed to know that she wasn't going to be tortured by shame by being associated with him forever. That she would be in his Wikipedia entry.

"Yes, I did." She licked her full, bottom lip. It was still swollen from his kiss. He wanted to catch it between his teeth, but not as much as he wanted to move his lips lower and suck on her clit until she screamed. "It's better this way. For me."

"Really?" The pang of disappointment he felt that she hadn't hauled off and decided that she wanted to be married to him hurt a little bit more than he could process right then. She wound her hand behind his neck, catching the hair at the back of his head through her fingers.

"I hope it's better for both of us."

"We won't be able to get the annulment now." He rested his head against the door, and her lips pressed against the center of his chest. "Are you really okay with that?"

"Now that we're on board with the story, we have more control." The idea that they were a team in this loosened the band that had formed around his chest. They were going to figure this out. Together.

"I'll think of a way to spin this so that it doesn't hurt your career. I promise." He only hoped he could keep that promise. But not hurting her might as well have been part of his wedding vows. Vows he didn't remember.

"Once the reporter found out, that cat was out of the bag." Her voice shook, so he pulled back and looked down at her. Her eyes were glistening with tears. He couldn't have that, not at all. "Who do you think told him?"

"Maybe the waiter? We weren't exactly discreet at the restaurant."

She nodded and looked down and he grasped her chin in his palm.

"What can I do?" He held her face between his two hands, not wanting her to hide from him. She didn't show emotions to very many people, and up until now, he'd only caught glimpses of vulnerability from her. That she was showing him this must have meant the she was finally opening up to him. Or that her feelings were so big that they were bound to spill out anyway.

"I've been thinking that I don't want—"

Please stay. That selfish wish he kept inside. The last thing he wanted to do was frighten her. "What don't you want, gorgeous?"

"I don't know if I can do this."

"Be married to me out in the open?"

"No." She tried to pull her face from his hands, but he didn't let her. They stared at each other for a long beat. And she didn't have to say what she was thinking. He knew from watching her that morning, the way she'd moved from his bed stiffly. The look on her face when she'd rehearsed.

Ballet was done with her, and she didn't know how to say the words yet.

"It's okay." He kissed her forehead. "It will be okay."

She subverted his expectations yet again when she pulled him down to her mouth.

This time, she was claiming him. He stayed still, let her explore his mouth, bite his lips. Sweep her tongue in search of his. She whimpered and wrapped her legs around his waist. He palmed her ass over the leggings and leotard she wore. He wanted to be pressing his fingers into that firm skin, and must have made a frustrated noise.

His cock was so full from being this close to her. Her eyes, her smell, the ways she rocked her center against his cock in perfect rhythm, fucking him through his clothes.

When she ran her greedy lips across his cheek, making his beard hairs stand up straight, he opened his mouth, somehow knowing she needed him to talk. To say things so filthy that she could completely leave her body. "Is this what you need baby? You need to ride my cock?"

She bit his ear in response.

"You're wild today, aren't you?" He pulled her thigh off his waist, needing her clothes the fuck off. "I'll never forget the feel of you sliding up and down my cock so hard your ass bounced."

He pulled off her leggings, ending up in a kneeling position in front of her. He couldn't help but take the fabric covering her pussy in between his teeth. Fuck. She smelled so ready for him. He didn't bother to take the leggings completely off. She wasn't going to have to move, and by the time he was done eating her, she'd barely be able to walk.

He picked her up. "You could wait until I took my shoes off." Her breathy voice made his cock chafe against his boxers and jeans. She needed this as much as he did. It was all too much for her—thinking about the thing her life was about disappearing. Falling without a safety net, just waiting to hit the ground.

But she didn't realize that he was on the ground, that he'd hit rock bottom long ago, and that he was right there to catch her.

"I don't need to wait until your damned shoes are off." He was grateful that she had a private dressing room and a couch. He needed to lay her out and to give her the kind of licking she needed. He dropped her on the couch and ran his fingers over her seam. Her leotard was all wet, and he could almost taste her on his mouth. "And you don't need to dance. Or to move right now."

"I don't?" He kissed her half-smiling mouth, and rubbed his index finger against where her nipples stood out against fabric. That must have felt good, because she arched her back and thrusted her hips at him. "Did you lock the door?"

"You shouldn't be thinking about who might walk in on us, gorgeous." He got up and flipped the latch, even though he said, "It doesn't matter that they can't get in. They're about to hear you screaming."

He made it back to her in two steps and dropped to his knees. Her leggings kept her from getting her legs too far apart, but he ran his hands up her thighs, worshiping the soft skin and the supple muscles there.

When he looked up at her, her gaze was glazed over and her chest moved up and down so fast she might have been performing. No, when she was performing, she made everything look effortless. It was only after that she showed the strain. What she was feeling right now wasn't strain. It was lust, for him.

They might be stuck in this marriage a little longer than she'd wanted to be, but he would never get enough of her. And he would make sure that it was worth her while.

He pulled the thin straps of her leotard over her shoulders. When her breasts popped out from the built-in bra, he paused and kneaded them until she gasped. "Hurry up."

"Do you have to get back to rehearsing?" He stilled his hands.

She blinked as though she'd forgotten where she was for a moment. "N—no. We're done for the day."

"Then, I'm going to take my fucking time." He bent and pulled one nipple into his mouth. Her eyes closed, and she moaned. Her entire body got involved when he gave her pleasure, and he fucking loved that. She was so fucking pretty straining up towards him. He must have done something good in the life before this one. His misspent youth was clearly not what had earned him this woman.

When the sounds she made got anxious and needy, he finished pulling down her leotard. She lifted her hips eagerly, so he could get it over her ass and all the way down. Somehow, he got it off one leg and tangled with her leggings.

He was only kind of kinky, but there was something deeply satisfying about having her all spread out in front of him, almost naked, but bound. She looked at him with a hungry gaze, and he felt like he was going to come in his jeans. He didn't even care. He just wanted to make her happy. Just wanted to make her body sing. Wanted to make her forget all her troubles and drown in the lustful dance they were in together.

"Touch your nipples." When she hesitated, he said, "I know that gets you hot enough to come all on its own, and I want to see it."

"You're not going to—" She snaked her hand down her belly, and he caught it with his.

"I'm going to when I'm good and ready, and when you're good and ready." He moved her hand to her breast, and she put the other one where he wanted it. "That's a good girl."

"You're a fucking tease."

"You want to talk about a tease?" She nodded. "Close your eyes. That first night we went out to dinner, you knew I was into you, yet you treated me like I was an inconvenience." He ran one finger against the seam where her thigh met her pussy. She shivered and grasped her nipples. "Good girl. I'd never felt like that, like I had a hill to climb when it came to a woman. Treating me like that after *you* came on to *me* was more than I could stand."

He let himself lower his head to where he wanted to be—always—for one taste before he continued. "Then, you flirted with that fucking waiter."

"I can talk to who I want. Just. Friendly."

Her head was thrown back then, and she was close. Simply from the sound of his voice and her touching her nipples. She jumped when he licked between her thumb and forefinger. "Of course you can, but you didn't even want to look at me."

She looked at him then with such lust. "Please."

He rubbed her opening with his thumb, brought that thumb up to her clit and rubbed. The fact that he'd gotten her that close with just talking, bare ghosts of touches had him almost as close to coming as she was. "Shhh. Good girl." She narrowed her gaze when he said that, and he knew she'd take her revenge.

He smiled at her, wanting to commit the giddy, desirous, vengeful look on her face like a treasured photograph. Then he dipped his head into her lap to take his fill.

* * * *

Charlie was determined to give her as many reasons to hate him as he could. Ordering her around instead of fucking her. Making her beg for his mouth.

God, God, God. His mouth.

She broke almost immediately when he touched his tongue to her clit. It was painful and pleasurable, and all too much. Shaking and arching from the sparks of everything he made with his lips and tongue. She moved her hands from her tortured nipples, and grabbed at his hair.

"Stop. Don't stop." She pulled and he finally looked up at her.

"Enough?"

She didn't know what to say to that. Now that he wasn't attempting to lobotomize her with an orgasm, she wanted him inside her, over her. And this time, she wanted him face-to-face.

But even more than that, she wanted him in her mouth. She hadn't gotten that last night. "Stand up."

He got up, and she scooted to the edge of the couch, where she was eye level with his cock. She was tempted to tease him in the same way that he'd teased her. And now that they had time together, she was going to make him jack off in front of her some time.

She undid his belt, and pushed his jeans and boxers down his thighs. Instead of making him wait, she took him in her mouth, as deep as she could, wrenching sounds from him that resonated inside her to her bones. Her hair was all up in a bun, so he couldn't wrap it around his fist the way he had the night before when he'd been riding her from behind.

"You don't have to do this."

She wanted to do this. Needed to make him as crazy and helpless as he'd made her. Tasting him, feeling this close to him kept her body ready for him, but she didn't store condoms in her dressing room and didn't know if he carried them around.

Fuckboy Charlie would have had condoms. Her husband, Charlie, on the other hand might not.

He cupped the side of her head as she sucked him in and jacked him off. When he'd been on his knees for her, she'd forgotten all the confusing feelings she was having about her future. The only thing that remained were her confusing feelings about him.

Sucking him off made even those feelings go away. Her only objective was to make him feel good, to wring helpless declarations, curses from his filthy mouth.

"Fuck, so good, gorgeous." She didn't look up at him, but felt his gaze on her face all the same. Every time she pulled off of him, she sucked in her cheeks. "Suck it like a good girl."

A prickle of anger hit her when he called her a good girl. She wasn't that, and she let him know it when she loosened her lips and ran her teeth across his cock.

"Fuuuuck." He gripped her jaw then, and she looked up at his face, expecting to see him pissed off. Instead, he was smiling. "You don't like it when I call you a good girl?"

She pulled back, and shook her head.

"What do you want me to call you then when you make pretty noises that almost make me come in my pants?"

She didn't answer, just licked the darkened head of his cock.

"You want to suck it and then not have me tell you how good you are?"

Using her hands, she took him deeper. She didn't know what to say to him. Although she wanted him to keep talking, dirty talk was not her strong suit.

He pulled his cock out of her mouth. "No more until you tell me what you want."

"You don't want a blow job? Fine." She would have gotten up, but his hands on her shoulders held her down.

"I want a blow job, but I want you to talk to me even more."

She swallowed, her throat suddenly hoarse. "I want to suck your cock."

"But you don't want me to call you a good girl?"

"No."

"Why not?"

She wasn't going to tell him that being a good girl never got her anywhere. She'd become a principal dancer because she was a hard-ass bitch, impervious to pain. And having Charlie see any of her softness, any of her dark insides was way too much. She didn't want him to call her a "good girl" because it felt so good when he did it.

"Call me whatever you want."

He tapped his cock against her lips and she opened her mouth. "You're going to tell me why eventually." She took him in, and snaked one hand between his thighs to touch his balls. She was probably imagining the emotion in his voice when he said, "Suck it, wife."

Chapter 10

It had been four years, three months, and six days since Charlie had spoken to his father over the phone. When he went to visit his brother and sister-in-law at Northwestern Memorial Hospital the day his youngest nephew was born two-and-a-half years ago, the schedules had gotten messed up, and he'd come face-to-face with his father.

Joseph Laughlin had nodded his head, turned, and walked out of the waiting room. Charlie's mother patted his arm, but then hurried after her husband. The years since seeing his father hadn't faded the ache in his chest that he felt every time he thought of his family.

Picking up the phone to tell his father he was married made him realize why he'd been yearning to settle down over the past couple of years. He'd thought it had been because he'd gotten to hold his nephew. But really, it was about wanting to feel like he belonged to someone.

And it wasn't like what he'd done was that bad. He'd gone out on his own, and done some sleazy shit. It was the fact that he'd done it publically, and it reflected poorly on his family. The Laughlin family name was everything to Joe-the-third.

For a hundred years, the Laughlins had owned the most respected newspaper in the Midwest. And, under his father's leadership, the family business had grown to include newspapers and local television stations all over the country. Joe had been able to grow in a business that most people were failing at.

Charlie's hands shook as he entered his father's direct office line. He would be a man and not send news of his wedding in an email to his whole family, which was the only way he'd communicated with his father for those four years, three months, and six days.

His father picked up on the third ring. "What do you want?" He would take offense, but that was the only way his dad had ever answered the phone. Even when they were little kids. "I wanted to tell you that I got married."

Joe appreciated communications being right to the point.

"Is she a porn star or a centerfold?"

That would have been a safe assumption when he was in his early twenties. Several of the girls on the *The Single Guy* had gone on to illustrious careers in adult entertainment. And with the benefit of years, Charlie had often wondered if he'd altered their lives in a bad way, but he tried to shake it off. Coming from a place of shame was not the right way to approach his father.

"Neither. She's a dancer."

"Oh, for Christ's sake." Charlie could see his dad shaking his head and patting himself down for a cigarette—a habit he'd given up when his sons were still small—from a thousand miles away. "You married a stripper?"

"Not a stripper. A principal dancer with the Miami City Ballet." His father was silent. "Laura Delgado."

"When did this happen?"

"A few months ago."

"And you're just calling me now?" Joe was probably standing now, looking out the window of his office on the deep-brown colored Chicago River. "Your mother is going to kill me when I have to tell her."

"You don't have to tell her. I'll call her myself."

"It's going to break her heart that she wasn't at the wedding."

"It wasn't big. Just me and her."

"How'd you convince her to do it?" Charlie winced. He had enough shit boiling in his head about why Laura shouldn't want to be with him. He didn't need his baggage with his dad making this any harder.

"I got her drunk." He went with the truth, and exactly what his father would expect. "And, miraculously, she wants to keep me." *For now.*

"I just wanted to tell you because there's going to be a story in a magazine."

"One of my magazines?"

"Nope. *Ocean Drive.*"

The phone clicked, and he was almost relieved. He wouldn't have to talk to his father for at least three more years.

* * * *

Lola looked smug, and Carla's shock was palpable. This wasn't nearly as difficult as telling her parents had been, but telling Carla that she had already been married to Charlie when she was trying to set her up with him was awkward to say the least.

Alana and Maya, her oldest cousin and cousin-in-law were in the kitchen getting wine. She'd only met Maya at the wedding—and judging from the short period of time she'd spent with the free-spirited painter—her cousin-in-law was going to think this was funny.

Alana, she wasn't as close to. Her oldest cousin had always been kind of intimidating. Smart, serious, worldly. Now that she was married to a guy she'd had a wild, New Year's Eve one-night stand with, she seemed to be a lot more fun.

"You married Charlie?" Carla's voice was more of a shriek.

"*Mija*, that's what she said." Grandma Lola with the helpful narrative.

"At my wedding?"

Laura still felt guilty about that. "I know it's like one of those memes on the Internet that had everyone up in arms about another person's wedding. It's gauche to steal focus. I'm sorry."

Carla stood up and moved to the couch next to her. "You don't need to apologize."

"It happened after you and Jonah made your exit. On the beach, I think. It was sort of wedding adjacent."

"I'm not mad."

"You should be."

"Wait a second. 'You think' it happened on the beach." Alana and Maya had four bottles of wine in between the two of them and glasses for everyone.

Laura shouldn't even be thinking about drinking any. She had just a few weeks of rehearsal left, and a very skimpy red costume to look magnificent in.

"I was a little drunk."

Carla squinted her eyes. "I don't think I've ever seen you drunk."

"I was injured and on a tropical island."

"And you fell in love at first sight." Lola was wrong, of course. Lust maybe. And she liked Charlie, which was growing to be a problem. She found herself wanting to see him at least once a day.

"Love at first sight is not a thing."

Her grandmother stood up. "Of course it is, look at this one." She gesticulated at Alana with her full wineglass, almost spilling. "And Carlita."

"It was not love at first sight. I thought he was an asshole." Carla whispered in her ear. "I only considered him more than a weekend thing after my dad gave him a black eye."

"And you were knocked up." Maya smirked over the rim of her glass. "I believe in love at first sight."

"You do?" It seemed surprising. Her cousin Javi's woman seemed to be about as cynical as Laura. She thought that was why they'd hit it off.

"Of course I do." Maya shrugged. "Why else do you think I acted like a lunatic about Javi for five years?"

"You were never a lunatic," Alana said. "And it wasn't love at first sight for me and Cole. It was more like lust-plus at first sight. And tequila shots. Lots of tequila shots."

"I challenged Charlie into doing shots. I remember that."

Alana laughed. "Well, then there's your answer."

Carla nodded sagely. "The women in our family should apparently never do tequila shots."

"Weren't you drinking beer the night you accidently got knocked up?" Maya was ready to read everyone for filth, apparently.

"She's right." Carla filled up her wineglass. "Whatever you do, don't drink beer and then fuck Charlie seven times with expired condoms."

"Noted."

"Laura, you should just admit that you're in love with him now." Lola smiled. "It will save your brothers from having to give him a bloody nose." Laura drew her finger across her throat in her grandmother's direction. Instead of shutting her mouth, her grandmother mimicked her and said, "This. What is this?"

"Do you want your secret to get out?"

Lola had the temerity to try to look disdainful. "Secrets? I have no secrets."

Laura wasn't sure why she said it now. Maybe it was because she was among women that she trusted, that she felt like she fit in with. Maybe it was because the glaring spotlight on her love life was getting to be too much. But, when she opened her mouth, she said, "I caught Lola making out with my *abuelo*." She looked down at the upholstery between her and Carla. "On this couch."

"*Tia* Lola, getting it in." Carla stood up and gave Lola a high five.

Seriously, did nothing shock these people?

"I told you I have no secrets."

"But aren't you worried that you'll hurt him again?" He looked reasonably happy when he was here the other day, but during most of her childhood, he'd been quiet and reserved. A trait he'd passed down to Laura's mother.

"Your *abuelo* is a big boy. We are just having fun." Lola poured herself more wine. "Isn't that why you were sneaking in when you caught us?"

Carla hit her upper arm so hard it stung. "You're sleeping with Charlie?"

"He's my husband." She didn't want to talk about how much she was growing to like her husband. Nor did she want to get into the fact that he was as addictive as an opioid, with the way he controlled her body and made her beg.

"But I thought you wanted to get an annulment?" Alana, always the lawyer. "You can't do that if you're actually fucking your husband. That was a question on the bar exam."

"That's what we were going to do at first. But then, that reporter showed up, and we decided we'd stay married. For now."

Carla hit her again, this time on the thigh. Probably hard enough to leave a bruise. "You weren't even going to tell anyone?"

"That was the plan. It was embarrassing." Her cheeks heated even now. "But it was a dumb plan. We're going to get a divorce."

"But for now you're dating your husband? And then you're going to divorce him?" Maya raised her eyebrows and took a long pull of rosé. "That sounds like a solid plan."

This time, Carla tapped her glass against Laura's. "Just remember the thing I said about beer and old condoms."

Lola smiled smugly from her armchair as Laura plotted undetectable ways of killing her.

Chapter 11

Laura didn't know why she'd come to Charlie's house after rehearsal. The actual dancing had been going better, but everything still hurt. The hurting put her in a shit mood, and the thought of not seeing him made everything feel worse. And, if they were going to have a relationship, even a fling, he'd see her at less than her best from time to time.

And less than her best she was. She sat on his couch with ice packs strapped to her knees with ace bandages over grey sweatpants that she'd pilfered from one of her brothers a decade ago. She wasn't sure which one—probably Max because Joaquin had never done sports. They had multiple holes, and she wasn't sure if the holes were from moths or from how much she'd loved them over the years. She may not be very close to either of her brothers now, but having Max's old sweats comforted her.

After the group class in the morning, she hadn't had time to see the trainer before rehearsing *Carmen* all afternoon. She'd gritted her teeth and gotten through, but even getting worked on for a half hour after the marathon rehearsal had ended wasn't enough to keep her from hobbling to her car. She hadn't even changed or showered. So, on top of looking like an old woman from the waist down, she stunk.

And her hair was a mess, too. She patted down the flyaways, and then stopped herself. She couldn't care this much about how Charlie thought she looked. He was her fake husband, totally temporary. But she liked how he looked at her and was afraid that if he saw her like this, he wouldn't want her anymore.

She didn't even know why she was there. When he'd given her a key, she'd been sure that she'd never use it. But the pull of seeing him, just being in his space was growing stronger for her with each passing day.

It was so weird that they were in the most serious kind of relationship possible, but they hadn't seen each other at their worst. They still had all the lust and good feelings, and none of the real issues. Everything still felt exceptional. Nothing was normal.

Soon, he would see that she was broken and fragile. And she didn't allow anyone to see her like that. Not even Lola, which made living with her grandmother stressful. But, as much as her grandmother had professed that she was never going back to Cuba, Laura didn't trust that Lola would stay at this point.

After trying and failing to read one of the fantasy novels that lined Charlie's bookshelves, she turned on the television. Just sitting around, watching something, wasn't a luxury she had allowed herself. Her parents had never had a television, and she'd never felt like entering the fray of what to watch among the other dancers at school, so she'd never gotten attached to any shows.

If her failing body forced her to retire, she'd have plenty of time to sit on a couch and watch television. At twenty-eight she would have decades to learn the art of the binge watch. She flipped channels until she saw a familiar shock of red hair and her cousin's raspy, laughing voice.

Carla was cajoling Jonah on camera about wanting to see some architectural feature in Rome. He was bitching because he wanted gelato. They were so funny together on-screen, and their chemistry was electric as Carla explained the history of some half-destroyed temple. Jonah merely grumbled along like a big toddler until they found a gelato stand. After that, the only grumbling came when some guys on the street hollered something vulgar at Carla.

Laura had never understood why people watched travel shows before. Not until halfway through the second episode of what looked like a marathon. Why not just go someplace? But this was actually entertaining. And, if people couldn't afford to travel, it gave them a bigger picture on the world.

And for the hour and half she sat in Charlie's dark living room, watching his work, she forgot how much her knees ached. It wasn't until a key turned in the lock, and footsteps sounded on the foyer floor that she remembered to feel self-conscious again. She moved to grab the remote and turn off the program. It was weird that she was watching Charlie's program while sitting in his house, waiting for him. Wasn't it?

She was a few seconds too late. He leaned over the back of the couch and kissed the side of her neck. As though this tableau was a totally normal sort of thing. If they had a real marriage, this *would* be normal.

"This is one of my favorite episodes." He hadn't moved away when he caught a whiff of her, so that was saying something. If he'd only been interested in sex with her, her odor certainly would have turned him off.

"It is?"

He brushed his hand over her shoulder and the bare skin of her chest. A bolt of electricity went up and down her spine as she melted into his casual touch. "Yeah, Jonah convinced us to shoot in Croatia. He'd been there on vacation a few times and wanted to show people that it wasn't what they'd seen in the early '90s on the evening news anymore. There's still evidence of the war, but it's beautiful, and the wine is plenty."

His wistful tone made her wonder if he was leaving something out. Had there been a woman in Croatia? Was sleeping around while he was travelling sort of his thing? She hadn't been able to find any pictures of girlfriends online, not after his disastrous first marriage, so maybe he just kept things off shore?

Her body stiffened, and he seemed to sense it. It was then that he noticed the melted cold packs on her legs.

"Are you okay?"

She certainly wasn't going to tell him that she was worried that he'd slept with every woman in Croatia. And Rome. And how many other shows had they done in the past year? Her knees had stopped throbbing, but a jealous little bird was inside her head, flapping its wings off.

"I'm fine."

He straightened up and moved towards the kitchen. "Are you sure? I think I have some pain relievers in the kitchen."

His mentioning pills doused her jealousy in a split second. "No. I don't take pills."

"Not even a Tylenol? Or an ibuprofen?"

"They don't really help in the long run, and they're not good for the heart."

"So you're just in pain all the time?"

Yes. That was her way of life. Choosing blind devotion to dance had been a terrible way to keep from becoming her mother. But she knew that she had never wanted to rely on two things—pills or a man—for her to feel okay.

Sure, she knew that over-the-counter pain relievers were a completely different beast than the pills her mother's "doctor" prescribed her. At first, they'd been for a fall she'd taken. Now, they were just to keep her steady. She also had pills for her nerves that Laura knew, but didn't want to know, could never be mixed with wine.

It had been such a relief to leave her parents' house to live at the academy. At eight, she shouldn't have been responsible for making sure her mom didn't overdose. Still, every time she visited, she surreptitiously flushed pills down the toilet. Her mother had never said anything to her, and Laura had the feeling that her father had taken to hiding and doling out the pills once Laura had left. Laura was only getting rid of the stash he hadn't found.

She touched her cheek, remembering the time she'd tried to tell her father that her mother had a drug problem.

He'd slapped her so hard that her jaw still had a click to it. After that, she hadn't tried to tell anyone else. The price was too high.

"Hey, where did you go?"

She hadn't realized she'd drifted into thoughts in the past until Charlie sat down next to her with a bottle of water.

"I'm right here." She smiled at him, grateful that he'd caught her before she'd fallen into melancholy. "Thank you."

"Have you eaten?"

She looked at the phone sitting next to her, surprised by how late it was. "No."

Turning his body toward her, he grabbed her shoulder. It was another pedestrian touch, not meant to be arousing, but everything with him turned her on. It was just lust, she tried to remind herself. It would fade, and they would go their separate ways. They would get a divorce, and be friendly exes when they had to see each other around Carla and Jonah. It would all work out fine.

Her hormones were not convinced. Unconsciously, she leaned into this man who had ruled her senses the other night.

"How about you grab a shower, and I'll fix us something to eat?"

"You cook?"

He smirked. "I don't burn boiled water."

When he stood up, he held out his hand to help her. Although she was feeling kind of used up these days, she could have gotten off the couch herself. Before sleeping with Charlie, she would have slapped his hand away. She prided herself on not expecting anyone to help her with anything.

But when she took his hand, it was as though something clicked into place inside her chest. His sincere smile warmed her in a way that full-on sex hadn't managed to in ages. At least not before this man. Sure, she wanted Charlie, but she was also starting to like him.

He didn't comment when she moved with stiff legs toward the bathroom, which she appreciated.

"Anything you don't eat?"

"Nothing that's not veggies and fish or chicken."

"Such an exciting palate, you have."

It couldn't hurt to let him in a little bit, and telling him why her diet was so restrictive was so minor that she felt like she could let it go. "Training diet."

He didn't respond until she was halfway down the hallway to the bathroom in his room. "If you wanted to cheat, I could help you work it off later."

* * * *

Charlie pulled the salmon out of the oven, leaving the parchment packages tied. When she turned the water off, he was throwing together a salad. If he hadn't heard her stomach gurgling on the couch, he would have joined her in the shower and made good on his promise to help her work up an appetite.

He didn't know why her reticence to tell him anything or accept anything from him turned her on. But it just made him want to know more about her. Maybe it was because he had to earn every damn thing with her that making her dinner felt like a holy mission.

Although he wanted to fuck her, ever since pulling into his driveway and seeing her car there unexpectedly, he wanted to make sure she was satisfied in every way. She'd looked so beautiful on his couch with nothing but the glow of the television lighting her features. He liked that she was in his home, watching his show. She was going to put on his T-shirt and eat his food.

And then he was going to kiss every inch of her body, and fuck her until she forgot that anything hurt.

She came into the kitchen wearing one of his dress shirts and a pair of sleep shorts she'd left there last week. He would not ask her where she'd gotten the men's sweatpants she'd been wearing before. That was something a jealous lover did. He had a strong impulse to rip them off her and fuck her on the counter, and that was another thing a jealous lover did.

He was not that man, and she would run away from him if he acted like that man.

"Smells delicious."

"You didn't give me a whole lot to work with, but I did what I could." *Lies.* He'd started keeping food she could eat at his house, hoping it would act like cheese in a mousetrap.

He slid a plate and another bottle of water in front of her before grabbing his own and sitting next to her. He'd moved the barstools closer, deliberately, and he was heartened when she didn't scoot away from him.

Barely, he resisted the urge to run his fingers through her wet hair. He couldn't wait to get close enough to smell his soap and shampoo all over her. And he didn't even stop his mind from assuming that she'd come to him with the intention of having sex again.

If she was just here for food and—he didn't know—comfort, he would give that to her. But his brain couldn't stop making up scenarios for how he'd touch her if she let him again. His wife was growing to be quite the sexual obsession. In most marriages, that might be a good thing, but he wasn't so sure that it was in their case. She could decide to pull the plug at any time given the circumstances of their union. He had the feeling that if he pushed her too hard to give him more, she would run fast and far.

She cleaned her plate in record time, and licked the corner of her mouth, where some dressing had landed.

"Thank you."

"My pleasure."

Silence stretched out between them. It was heavy and promising. Her obsidian-colored gaze bore into his for a moment before she gave him a once-over. He was in his uniform of dress-pants and a shirt like the one she was wearing, nothing spectacularly interesting, but he felt like he was being appraised. And, surprisingly for him, he liked it.

She licked her lips again, this time for no reason at all. He didn't move—wouldn't dare. If his wife wanted to seduce him with nothing but a look, he would let her.

Her gaze snagged on his lengthening cock, and he couldn't help but smirk when her eyes got wide and glassy. Almost tentatively, she cupped a hand over him. He groaned, and she looked back up over his face.

"Every time I see you."

She let out a light laugh. "Even when I'm stinky and in sweatpants?"

He nodded. "Even then." He huffed when she squeezed his cock even tighter. "Even more than when you're all dressed up."

"Why?" She must not be able to see how thoroughly enchanted he was with her. Maybe he had to demonstrate that through worshipping her body. Maybe she only understood emotion when it was backed up by movement. Maybe the whole ice queen thing wasn't an act?

"Because I can see you."

"And you like what you see?" She went to pull her hand away, but he grasped her wrist. He hated that she sounded so uncertain about him. Hated that he'd given her reason to.

"Every damned thing I see I like." He let her wrist go, stood in front of her and took her face between his palms. Her mouth formed a shocked "o" before he pressed his lips to hers.

She dug her fingers into his sides, spread her legs, and pulled him closer. Their bodies were flush, and he loved the feel of her against him, but he needed her on a flat surface.

He grabbed her thighs, which she latched around his hips and lifted her up. The counter was the closest horizontal spot, but it was covered in glasses and plates. He broke away from her mouth to make sure he wouldn't drop her—not sexy at all—on the way to the couch.

"I loved seeing you here when I got home." She didn't respond, just kissed him again. Maybe he shouldn't have said anything that sappy; he didn't want to scare her away. But he wanted her to know that he felt something for her that was beyond the fact that she made him hard whenever he caught a glimpse of her. Even though she was like his own personal, walking porn video, he wanted to hear her laugh almost as much as he wanted to bury himself inside her.

Once he'd gotten them both to the couch safely, he pressed her down with his pelvis, and she rewarded him with a moan of approval. He sat back on his haunches, and began unbuttoning her shirt.

He couldn't say anything because he was too busy looking at her and being happy that she belonged to him. For now, she was his girl.

"Say something." Her husky voice took him by surprise.

"You need me to talk to get off?" He reached the bottom button and opened his shirt. Her creamy skin called out for his tongue, but it wouldn't do if she needed him to talk so she could come.

She shook her head. "But I like it."

"I aim to please." So many filthy scenarios that he could lay out for her filled his mind. He had a hard time choosing just one. He took her nipples between the thumb and index fingers of his hands and she arched back. Her eyes blinked closed, and she gasped. "I love how responsive you are wherever I touch you."

He scooted back and moved one hand to her cotton panty-covered pussy. She pressed into his hand like she was offering herself up to him. "And when I touch you here, I like how you forget who we are and that this is all supposed to be fake." Too sappy because she stopped the lewd press of her crotch. "It makes me so hard to think of you getting all wet because I touched you."

He slipped his fingers between the band of her panties and her skin, and found her all ready for his cock. But it wasn't time yet. Soon, just not yet.

"When did you get this wet for me?" She didn't respond, so he moved his fingers back up to her nipples and pinched. "When?"

Her eyes blinked back open, her gaze full of fire and lust. She fucking slayed him. "When you touched my neck when you came in."

"That's when you got all soaking wet?" He slipped his hand back in her panties and pressed a finger inside her.

"Yes." Her voice came out as a hoarse whisper.

"Why didn't you ask to sit on my face right then, gorgeous?" She tightened around him more the dirtier his words got. He'd give her what she needed then. "I would have obliged, and licked you until you cried for me to stop."

"I needed to shower."

"I don't fucking care. If this pussy needs licking, I'll do it." He pressed his thumb to her clit and she squeezed her legs together. "Did you rub yourself in the shower?"

Her eyes shot open as though she'd been caught. "Y—yes."

He pulled his hand out of her and slapped her thighs open. "I don't like to hear that." He stood up to pull her panties off her legs. "Take the shirt off."

She wiggled it off and lay naked in front of him. "You too."

"Are you going to show me how your rubbed your clit if I do?" She nodded. When her hand wasn't in between her legs, working for an orgasm by the time he got his shirt open, he put his hands on his hips and stopped. "Then, do it. Show me how you like your pussy rubbed. I'll remember so that the next time you need to get off and I'm around, I'll do it for you."

She got to work between her legs and it barely speeded him up undressing. He had to keep his promise, to watch her do this to herself. It was so fucking hot, especially when she closed her eyes and the muscles in her forearm strained. She liked a hard touch.

When he felt like she was about to come—short breaths, quicker strokes—he sped up, pulling a condom out of his pants pocket. He'd known he wasn't going to make it to his bedroom with her tonight, so he'd grabbed one while she was in the shower. If he'd have known she needed to get off then—

Once he was naked and suited up, he said, "Open your eyes, Laura." This time she didn't hesitate. "Do you want to get off on your hand or my cock?"

"Both."

"Greedy girl." He crawled over her body, wincing when his dick nudged up against her belly. He took her mouth again, and she wrapped her arms around his neck. With one hand, he guided his cock to her entrance and pushed in. "Put your hand back down there, greedy girl."

When he felt her fingers making tight circles around her clit again, he sat up so he could watch her touching herself while he was deep inside her. He pulled her legs up in the air, so her ankles crossed behind his neck.

Between the clutch of her pussy, the brush of her fingers on every stroke, and the sight of her tightened up and close to breaking, he felt like he could barely hold on. He didn't even let himself zero in on the way her tits bounced every time he got all the way inside her. She was going to kill him for sure. Or maybe he was dead, and this was what heaven was like. He didn't deserve it, but he wouldn't stop himself from taking it.

He licked her calf and buried any earnest words in her skin when she tightened up around him and cried out. *Shit.* He needed to orgasm her at least one more time, but he couldn't hold out. She was too perfect.

He didn't just come; he exorcised demons in the moments that followed. He'd hadn't felt like he was at home anyplace in years. But inside Laura he felt a peace spread through him that came from the vicinity of his chest.

Instead of saying it, saying that he was starting to need her, he licked the skin stretched over her calf muscle and winked in the promise of debauching her further.

Chapter 12

Meeting the family had Charlie sweating through his shirt. It didn't help that it was ninety-plus degrees. Once Laura had told her parents about the wedding, they'd decided that they needed to throw a reception. Laura had talked them down from their country club to her cousins' parents' house.

He'd met most of the Hernandez family at the wedding. The Delgados—other than Laura—hadn't paid anyone else attention. Where the Hernandezes were loud and outspoken, the Delgados seemed much more reserved.

"Are you sure they don't already hate me?" He looked over at his wife, who seemed incredibly tense. Like, more than usual.

"They don't even really like me." She squared her shoulders, and he gave into the urge to put his hand on her back in a gesture meant to reassure her. She accepted his touch, and it felt like a victory. "They're too busy being miserable to hate anyone."

Laura had tried to explain her odd relationship with her family over dinner the other night. After the magazine had published the news about them two weeks ago, it had been a lot easier to convince her to spend time with him.

Almost every night that she didn't rehearse through the dinner hour, she came over to Charlie's house. He'd found out what she could eat and made sure he had it on hand, so he could feed her and fuck her most nights.

It hadn't taken long, but he'd grown addicted to this woman. He couldn't touch her enough. She was in the last stages of rehearsal before the ballet season began, so her body was exhausted. He woke up in the middle of the night wanting her, but had schooled himself into letting her sleep.

And she'd started opening up to him, too. She smiled more, gave him more of her story. Every tidbit she gave him—about rehearsal, her family, anything at all—made him want her more. The way she'd started to give him her touch and lay down some of the shit she threw up to keep other people away, made him feel like they had a chance of making this work.

Until morning, when he woke her up by kissing and biting the back of her neck, all along her spine. He liked to feel her come back from sleep in his arms. And it never took long for her to start writhing.

She'd made herself comfortable and started wearing his T-shirts to bed. She was so long and tall that they barely covered her ass. Most mornings, he couldn't even wait to get her naked before getting inside her.

If he couldn't convince her to stay married to him, he would have to burn his bed. Maybe demolish the entire house. Two weeks of her there, and he couldn't imagine living there without her soap smells in his bathroom, her pre-portioned meals in his refrigerator. The sounds she made when she was coming around his cock.

Thinking about Laura coming apart was not the way to meet her parents. They would definitely hate him if he walked in to his rush-job wedding reception with a hard-on.

She wrapped an arm around his waist. Over the past two weeks, the sex had gotten even better, as he'd gotten to know every nook and cranny of his wife's filthy mind. But she'd gotten more affectionate with him, easy. He didn't know if she realized it, but she'd started to reach out to him. And it felt amazing. He felt needed, like he belonged.

When the door opened, Molly Hernandez nearly ripped Laura out of his arms.

"You are the last one of your siblings I would have expected to elope." When she was done hugging Laura, she grabbed Charlie's hand and dragged him into the house. "You've got a good one here, though, you know?"

Laura looked up at him, and he thought for a second it was love in her gaze. "I do know he's good. That's why I had to snap him up, right away."

"Seems risky not even getting a taste of the goods first." Molly's South Boston accent was thick and laced with sarcasm. Charlie's skin heated. "Your parents and brothers are out back. Joaquin is scowling at the paella his sous chef made, and Max is next to the bar, scowling into a whisky as usual. I don't think your mother's taken more than one Xanax, but the day's still young."

Laura's eyes widened and she grabbed onto his arm. He leaned over and whispered so that Molly wouldn't hear. "It's going to be okay. I've got you."

* * * *

Alejandro Delgado had the look of an El Greco painting about him. Long in the face, dour, very pale. Laura got her long, lean figure from him. And the color of his eyes was similar, but his gaze lacked the light and fire of his daughter's. Laura's mother, Sylvie Hernandez-Delgado, had once been beautiful. But she had the look of someone who wasn't there.

Neither of them had gone to Carla and Jonah's wedding. Apparently, the long-distance travel would have been terrible for Sylvie's "nerves."

Meeting them made him want to tackle his wife and run away. Running away from family had worked out to his advantage, and maybe they could make it a Delgado-Laughlin family tradition.

Instead, he shook hands with Alejandro and kissed the back of Sylvie's. A ghost of a smile crossed her face, which felt something like victory.

When she kissed both of her mother's cheeks and embraced her father, Laura had that same pained look she got when she thought no one was looking after rehearsal. Charlie wrapped his arm around her shoulders while they all stared at each other in awkward silence.

After a scan of the backyard, he spotted both of her brothers. Joaquin, an imposing bearded man, was next to the buffet table, and he spotted Max at the bar, just like Molly had told them. He had met Max and Joaquin Delgado at the wedding. They were both kind of quiet and surly. Growing up in this family, he could see why. Suddenly, he was filled with gratitude that Laura had found dance and gotten out of her house as a teenager. Even though dancing hurt now, back then it must have saved her.

"You're late." Laura's mother's voice was sing-songy and she trailed off at the end of her sentence. More silence until she looked down at Laura's left hand. "And, where's your ring?"

Charlie's face heated again.

"Reality television is not that lucrative." Alejandro's misguided statement was like a punch to the gut, reminding him about how he always felt around *his* father.

He squeezed Laura's shoulder when he felt her startle against him. Her father's oblique insults were sort of like gunshots.

"Actually, we just haven't had a chance to pick one out yet." He'd already bought a ring for his wife, but he was waiting to give it to her for another week. He planned to surprise her with the ruby and diamond ring on opening night of *Carmen*. Even if she divorced him, as planned, he wanted to give her something. He wanted her to wear his ring for as long as he could keep it on her finger. "She's been so busy with rehearsals. I get to watch sometimes because my company sponsored the show, and she's simply stunning in it."

"She's very old to be a ballerina." Charlie had never hit a woman, but he wanted to slap Laura's mother. Still, he kept his hand firmly rooted on Laura's shoulder. Even though she was clearly on something, she knew exactly where her daughter's vulnerabilities were and knew how to stick the knife in but good. "It's good that you have money to take care of her."

"I have savings." Laura turned to her father. "And, thanks to all your hard work, I have a trust fund."

"And now she has me." Charlie ignored how Laura's body recoiled at that remark. She might not like the fact that she could depend on him, but he sure as hell wasn't going to let her asshole of a father think that Laura was going to end up depending on him.

He had to get his wife away from her parents. The need to protect her overwhelmed his normally good manners, and he steered her toward the bar. Both of her brothers must have been looking out for Laura surreptitiously because they both appeared next to her.

Max had a glass of white wine poured for her. "Drink."

Laura took it, and swallowed down a gulp. "Thanks."

She smiled up at her brother. Max's beard-covered mouth tipped up at the edges. "Only way to deal with the both of them."

"Why did you even invite them?" Joaquin nudged Laura's shoulder. "He doesn't know how to be anything else but an asshole."

Anger flipped around in Charlie's stomach on Laura's behalf. She didn't deserve to get shit from her brothers just for wanting her parents to celebrate their marriage. As though she sensed him growing angry, she touched him lightly on the arm.

"He doesn't."

She looked down, and Charlie wanted to tip her chin up and see whether she was about to cry. If she were about to cry, he'd have her out of here so fast heads would blow off. "I just didn't want her to be left out."

"You're more tenderhearted than me," Max said.

Joaquin shook his head. "She didn't do a damn thing to stand up for me when he got going."

Laura reached out for her brother. "She couldn't. She was too—"

"I know, but that's not an excuse I accept." Joaquin's words were harsh, and Charlie knew that there was something behind them.

Listening in to them made him realize that as much as Laura had opened up to him, it wasn't enough to really know her.

* * * *

Laura couldn't breathe out in the backyard. The twinkly lights, the music, the free-flowing champagne were all so lovely. But it was all a big lie.

She couldn't explain why she hated Charlie standing up to her parents so much. Not even to herself. And having him hear her brothers talking about them was almost worse. So, after Carla had made a bawdy toast, scandalizing Laura's parents and delighting Lola and the Hernandez clan, Laura found the first-floor powder room and locked herself in.

She just needed a minute. A minute stretched to maybe fifteen after she sat on the closed toilet seat. She'd never forget how safe and secure she'd felt with Charlie's arm tight around her. He'd told her parents that he was going to buy her a ring, and she wanted that more than anything. *She wanted their marriage to be real.*

He wasn't the man she'd thought he was—feckless, irresponsible, full of empty promises and witty flirtation. Looking at him next to her father made everything he'd come to mean to her feel so real that it threatened to pull her under.

She could not fall in love with her husband.

Falling in lust with him had been bad enough. Letting herself go to him every night was even worse. Each morning, after she got in her car to drive to class, she promised herself that this would be the last night. She'd push him off when he asked if she was going to be out for dinner. But, when his text came in at around six thirty, never after six forty-five, she told him she was coming to him.

The two nights she'd had rehearsals that ran until eleven and gone to the condo she now apparently shared with *both* of her grandparents, she'd barely slept. Not until she'd given in and dug out Charlie's T-shirt from her bag. She needed his smell against her skin to go to sleep.

All of that, plus him standing up for her, brought a knot of tears from her chest, and she leaned over and sobbed.

She must have been way too loud because someone knocked on the door.

"*Mija*, it's Lola."

"Go away."

"No."

Laura stood up and yanked the door open. When Lola saw her tear-streaked face, she closed the door behind her. "What happened?"

She'd enjoyed having her grandmother around for the past few months—until Lola had interfered and ruined her life. And seeing the contrast between her mother and her mother's mother tonight set of a spark of rage inside Laura's chest. Maybe none of this would have happened if Lola hadn't abandoned her family years ago. Coming back into their lives now was too little, too late.

"Go. Away." That's all her grandmother was good at, anyway. She'd certainly had an easy enough time leaving her mother. And her grandfather. Her poor *abuelo*, who she was now stringing along. And now she'd come here, and made her feel things. Laura had survived by never allowing herself to feel. Now, she'd been pushed into falling in love, when she'd never intended to. "Go back to Havana."

Lola's gaze darkened and she seemed to get a few inches taller. "I'm not going anywhere."

"You've messed everything up by coming back."

"*Lo siento, mi amor.*"

"It's too late for you to be my grandmother. I don't need you anymore." She only needed herself—not her grandmother, definitely not Charlie. That was the only way.

Lola wiped at the skin under Laura's eyes. Her mascara must have run. Even though she couldn't let herself trust it now, she'd needed this her whole life. Maybe if Lola hadn't stayed in Cuba, everything would have been different. Maybe her mother would have grown a backbone like Lola's. Maybe she wouldn't have married her father at all.

"I'm so sorry, sweet girl."

Tears threatened again. "I wish—"

"What do you wish?"

"It's nothing."

"You're crying in the bathroom at your wedding reception. It's something." Lola let her go, and pointed at the closed toilet seat. "Sit."

Laura obeyed because her grandmother's tone brooked no objections, and Lola hefted her handbag onto the counter and wetted a washcloth.

"I wasn't going to tell you this. I wasn't going to tell anyone this. Not even a priest." She wiped down Laura's face. It was soothing, and she couldn't help but accept her grandmother's kindness. "But I had my reasons for not moving here. They weren't good reasons, but they existed. I told myself that I wasn't going to explain why I'd hurt all of you. That I would just try to make it up to you."

"Why?"

"Because, even after what he did, I did not want to hurt or embarrass your *abuelo*."

Laura got a sick feeling in the pit of her stomach, as though her body knew she'd been wrong about Lola before her mind did.

"But now that I see how much damage I did—" Lola put down the cloth and rooted around in her purse until she pulled out a cosmetics bag. "Not just to your mother. But to you and your brothers. . ."

"We're all okay." It was a lie, but she wanted to make things okay for her grandmother. Not because she had any reason other than her intuition that Lola wasn't completely at fault for her fucked up family.

"Your grandfather and I had a great deal of passion for one another."

Her mind flashed to the image of her grandparents making out on the couch like teenagers and she cringed. "Believe me, I'm aware."

That got a sharp bark of laughter out of her grandmother. "We should not have gotten married. I'm glad we did, because none of you would be here if we hadn't. But, I wanted to be free, and he wanted a wife who would do his bidding."

"Sounds like some other people we know."

"Well, your mother and I never had very much in common. She was so sure that I was the worst wife ever." Lola smoothed some cream blush across Laura's cheeks—she'd become a cosmetics junkie since moving to the United States. "And, really, I just had interests other than housekeeping and talking to small children."

"She used to tell us that we were lucky that she was around so much." Laura closed her eyes so her grandmother could sweep on a light coating of eyeshadow. "I always wished that she had more to do."

"Your grandfather wasn't happy with me, and he found someone else." Laura blinked open her eyes, and saw the sorrow etched across her grandmother's face. "I loved him so much, and I became so furious that I refused to listen to him say another word to me."

"So, you didn't leave when he found the opportunity to?"

"He wanted to come here to be with *her.*"

"That bastard." She felt nauseous. Her sweet, little old grandfather was a filthy *philanderer.* Her grandmother's behavior all those years ago made sense, and Laura felt guilty for lashing out a few moments ago. "You certainly seem to be ready to talk to him now."

"It's been thirty-five years." Lola shrugged, and her lips curled. "That woman is dead."

"So?" If Charlie ever cheated on her, she would never be able to look at him without thoughts of murder again. *Shit.* That had happened fast. "Aren't you still angry with him?"

"Of course I am, but love is more complicated than that."

Laura shook her head, hoping to dislodge thoughts she didn't want to have. She wouldn't say she was in love—not out loud—but having a relationship was somehow a lot more complex than having a sham marriage or a quickie annulment had been.

"You've forgiven him then?"

Her grandmother stroked the side of her face gently. It was patronizing, but the woman was old. She'd earned the right to be patronizing. "It's been a long time. Neither of us have forever to be used on holding grudges. I've just found that it's much more pleasurable for me to let things go and enjoy what we have."

It all sounded so simple. Let go. Enjoy what was right in front of her.

"I can't do that with Charlie." Laura sighed and stood. "We have the rest of our lives to plan for, and I don't want to promise him things I can't give him."

"Who says you can't give him what he wants?"

"I can't just quit and let him protect me. I have to fight my own battles. Live my own life."

"You're afraid of becoming like your mother?"

Yes.

"It's not that. We're just too different. We don't make sense."

"Some of the best things in life don't make sense."

"Like affairs with one's ex-husband?" Laura wanted to get out of the room. The tiny room was getting stuffy with two people and major life decisions all crammed in there together.

"That's not what I meant." Lola put her hand on Laura's shoulder, making it known that she would stay right there until she'd dispensed all the grandmotherly wisdom that she could tolerate. "He's not asking you to give anything up. The way he looks at you is rare, and precious. The only thing you'll be giving up if you end things with him is that. And I want you to have that."

"I can't dance for much longer." She didn't know why she'd confessed now. Or to her semi-estranged grandmother. But those words had been floating around in her brain, her muscles, and on her heart for so long that they were going to leak out sooner or later. "I have to know what I'm going to do next before I commit to anything. And Charlie wants all of me. Right now. It's scary."

Lola pressed one her of fingers against Laura's breast bone. "All that he wants is in here. You'll figure the rest out."

"But didn't you hear me?" The organ in her chest ached and shifted when Charlie was near her, when he took care of her like she meant something more to him. It was an unfamiliar feeling and she wanted to bottle it up and push it away all at the same time. "I'm afraid."

"That's the reason to do it, *mi amor.*" She turned and open the bathroom door. "Love is the only reason to do anything in this life."

Chapter 13

Laura went outside and played the part of a blushing bride after that. She joked with her brothers and cousins and drank one too many glasses of champagne. She looked at her husband, and saw what her grandmother had described. And it didn't make her cringe back into herself. She allowed the feelings that flowed from Charlie—as easy as summer afternoon rain—inside her. It was almost like an experiment, and it was a successful one until they were alone in the car.

He had his hand on her leg, squeezing gently through her dress. And it was like they were any other couple headed to their shared home after a family party. He hadn't asked her if she was going to sleep over; it was assumed. She had a freaking toothbrush at his house. And a drawer.

Her husband's contentment was palpable, and she knew it didn't have anything to do with the slew of gifts they'd received from her family. Although she would have liked to imagine that his happiness came from the naughtier gifts that Alana, Carla, and Maya had given her in private—the ones that made her blush to think about—she knew it wasn't that either. He fit in drinking scotch and smoking cigars with her Uncle Hector. He had lugged the rapidly growing toddler Layla around, and he even seemed to understand her mumbled toddler-speak.

A pang in her heart at the thought of Charlie with a baby made her push his hand off of her leg. She didn't want all of this to become so normal, so much a part of her that it would hurt when it ended. She struggled to separate this into pieces in her mind.

"What's wrong?" He glanced over at her as he moved through traffic.

"Nothing."

He laughed, and she knew he wasn't buying it. "You know, up until just then, I didn't really feel married."

She scowled at him. "Why not?"

"I just remember Jonah telling me a story about how the word 'nothing' had about a thousand meanings that he didn't realize until he hooked up with Carla."

"Hmm." She looked out the window of the car, and tried to lose herself in the bright lights and passing cars. Willed Charlie into companionable silence.

"And 'nothing' doesn't mean 'nothing,' right now." He sighed and tapped the steering wheel with one finger, after they stopped behind a line of cars waiting to exit the freeway. "Is it your parents?"

"No. It's nothing." Nothing that she wanted to talk about. She needed to get her own head straight before word-vomiting all over Charlie. He acted like it was so easy, that they could just be married and date and fit into each other's lives. She felt like she was the only person in this car actually thinking about the consequences of what they were doing, the only one thinking about the future.

"See, I don't believe you, gorgeous." He put his hand on her thigh again, and she didn't bother to move it this time. "Is it me? Did I do something wrong?"

"No." That was the truth. He was the perfect husband, and that was the problem. "You did everything right."

"Then, why aren't you talking to me?"

"I'm just thinking, okay?"

"Don't you know?" He slid his hand up her thigh. "I want to know what you're thinking about. I want to know everything that goes on in your head. I want to know what's hurting you so that I can fix it. It's sort of become an obsession."

If she were a different kind of woman, his words would have wrapped themselves around her heart so tightly that she wouldn't have been able to live without him repeating them. But she wasn't capable of the kind of openness that he demanded from her. The sooner he saw that, the sooner he could let her go. And it was best for him to let her go.

"I can't give you that."

"Then what can you give me?"

"Sex." Even though, every time they had sex, she came closer and closer to cracking her heart open to him. If she were being honest with herself, she already had.

He moved his hand higher, until his little finger was nestled against the apex of her thighs. "Is that all you're willing to give me?"

His voice held a chord of hurt that she hated. She wanted to take it back and tell him that he could have whatever he wanted from her.

Before she could answer, he said, "I'm not going to turn it down, but guess what?"

She looked over at him, and his face was all in shadows and light. For the millionth time, she was struck by how gorgeous he was. He was Narcissus, of a sort that hadn't drowned. Instead of remaining an adolescent asshole and becoming irredeemable because of that stupid tape, he'd picked himself up. He was even more beautiful now that he had been just after college. There was something there that hadn't been there before. A determination that set his jaw in stark relief.

"What?"

He pulled the car into his driveway and shifted into park before turning to her. His gaze was intense, and she was tempted to flee the car. But she knew he would follow her. She'd been so worried about him burrowing inside her and making her fall in love with him. So afraid of losing herself in him. But he already had her pinned.

"I'm not going to stop trying to make you see that this works." He grabbed her knee, and put his hand under her dress. Her skin burned from the searing truth of his words paired with his savagely tender caress. "And if I have to make you see that through sex, all the better." He smiled, and the street light against his face made it look almost sinister. "That's the best weapon I have."

* * * *

Just sex his ass.

He knew when she'd disappeared for a half hour that there was trouble brewing. He could smell it like a thunderstorm rolling in off the Gulf. She didn't know that he knew that secret, that her emotions weren't as locked away from him as she thought. And he wasn't going to tell her that he knew.

She'd just given him an open invitation to show her how she felt about him. To give a mind-blowing demonstration of how magical they were together. He wasn't going to apologize for standing up for her with her parents. And he wasn't going to promise not to do it again. That wasn't a promise he could keep, and it contradicted his marriage vows.

Every day, those vows mattered more and more to him. They might be a temporary inconvenience for her, but he was going to stop questioning how right it felt to belong to Laura. He was going to do everything he could to make her stay. The only way he would let her leave was if he was sure that was the only way he could make her happy. Watching her walk away would gut him, but what she wanted was more important to him.

He got out of the car, and made it to the other side in time to help her out. She was unsteady on her feet even though she'd had maybe three glasses of champagne in three hours, and that filled him with a satisfaction that bordered on carnal. The fact that he could make this prima ballerina falter gave him a shot of manly pride.

That pride countered the feeling of vulnerability that chased him around when he was dealing with her emotions. Although he could predict when her mood was going off track, he couldn't seem to do anything to stop it. He couldn't lie back and let things happen to her. And he sure as shit wouldn't stand by and allow her parents to hurt her. He had to make her see they were a family now. And he wouldn't treat her like her father treated her mother.

He respected her as much as he wanted her.

She regained her grace and walked up the front path to his door provocatively. Although she had to be quite slim for her job, her curves were undeniable. The long lines of her body sang to him. It was no wonder to him that entire theaters of people teared up when she danced. With the flutter of her hand, she could make people hold their breath.

She was a conductor of a sort, but of emotions. She had him on a string, but she wouldn't admit that he meant anything to her—that what was happening between them was unique and important.

When they'd met at the wedding, her body had driven him crazy. Her wild eyes and supple lips, the strength in her movements when she'd pushed him into the sand and kissed him for the first time. He'd been helpless to stop her when she didn't know what she was doing.

Now? When she was deliberately twitching her hips in a way that made her skirt ghost across her bare thighs? He was a goner.

But now that he'd learned her body and knew exactly how to make her come apart in his arms over and over, for hours at will, he had a way to fight against it.

Instead of opening the door when he reached her, he pressed her against the wooden planks and took her mouth. She tasted like champagne and spice, and she opened to him without hesitation. He swept his tongue inside her mouth and there they danced. It was a fight, a play fight, but a battle nonetheless. But when he was touching her, and she was giving back to him this way, it didn't matter who had the upper hand. They were equals in this.

He'd kept his keys in his hand and got the door open without moving his mouth away from hers. He caught her by the waist and carried her into the foyer, not setting her down until they reached his bedroom.

Though he had a lot to say to her that *didn't have anything to do with sex*, he stuck with the only thing she was willing to offer him. "Panties off, gorgeous."

When she went for the straps of her dress, he knocked her hands away before kneeling down and pulling her underwear off, leaving her dressed. "You don't want me to be naked?"

"I always want you naked, but I've been thinking about this dress all night." It was made of some ultra-soft fabric that was almost the same smoothness as her skin. When she'd walked into his living room wearing it earlier, he hadn't been able to get the thought of sticking his head under it and eating her until she cried for him to stop out of his head. Everything she wore turned him into a sick bastard, and he wasn't even sorry. He couldn't even fake it with her.

"You haven't been thinking about it on your bedroom floor?" Her voice had this provocative thing that made him growl every time she did it. Her voice and her body had the same effect on him—drugging.

"I want to feel like I'm drowning in this dress while I lick this pretty cunt." He caught the back of her thighs when she wavered. In the past few weeks, he'd learned that she liked it when he used ultra-dirty words. It made her go soft and even wetter. He'd use the c-word every other word if it made her happy.

"Your funeral." Her soft laugh stopped when he crawled underneath her skirt. He kept his grip on the backs of her thighs as he kissed up her legs from the ankles. He'd never had fantasies about licking the shoes of a woman in high heels, but he could understand it when he was at her feet. He hoped those shoes were reasonably comfortable. Because after he licked her until she came, he wanted those pointy stilettoes digging into his ass as he rode her.

She must have been holding onto her thighs while he was making his way up her legs to her pussy because he encountered resistance getting there—he was stuck under her dress. And he hadn't meant that drowning thing literally. He nudged her until her fingers fought for purchase on the top of his head through the fabric. The desperation of her touch gratified him and sent more blood to his dick as the scent of her made saliva gather in his mouth.

Mrs. Hernandez had insisted that they have some of the cake she'd ordered for their wedding reception. But, as he ate a piece from his wife's hand, catching her index finger in his mouth, he'd only wanted this.

Her body jerked when his mouth finally made it to her pussy, but he held her upright. She moaned when he took her clit into his mouth, and he smiled against her folds as she tried to scalp him through her dress.

He wasn't letting her sleep tonight until her body knew who it belonged to. Even if he couldn't wring the words from her mouth, her pleasure would make it clear.

* * * *

Laura never would have guessed that a reformed misogynist pig would have learned to eat pussy like a fucking god, but miracle-of-miracles, her husband was a champion at it. And it wasn't fair to call him a misogynist, because he'd proven that title didn't fit anymore.

When he took her clit between his lips, brushing it with the edge of his teeth in a way he knew drove her crazy, she wasn't sure she could stay standing. But he held her up, and she wasn't about to pick an argument about it this time. Every time he did this—and he seemed to love doing it—her body became primed more easily. Even as she knew that she should be pulling away from him, her body wouldn't let her. Her senses tuned to his movements, and at this point, just a look or a touch could get her close to coming. The first time, it had just been his words, and now it was the touch and memory that had her spiraling into an orgasm with an unladylike screech.

Only when the last of her tremors had subsided did he break contact with his mouth and lower her to the edge of the bed. Still, he didn't come out from beneath her dress. He kissed up and down her thigh reverently, and she petted him. Although she didn't want to accept him soothing her, she wanted to give that to him.

She didn't know how long they were like that, but she finally pulled up her skirt. His hair was ruffled, and his beard was still wet with her. The power in being able to turn this man into the debauched picture in front of her had her needing him inside her.

"What?" He appeared to be as dazed as she was, and he hadn't even gotten off yet. He licked his lips as though he savored the taste of her, and it gutted her.

"I didn't want you to actually suffocate down there."

She gasped when he ran his fingers over her, nerve endings still ablaze.

"This? I could never suffocate down here." He entered her with one finger, just making the need worse. "This is ambrosia. It could keep me alive on a desert island." He withdrew his hand and licked his finger. She couldn't look away from the filthy way his tongue swirled around his finger. The same way it had moved against the most intimate part of her.

He stood up, and his hand stayed hers when she went for his belt. Instead, he pressed her to the bed with his body and scooted her up. His cock brushed against her bare pussy, and she whimpered. She needed him again.

"I'm going to fuck you. Don't worry."

"Who said I'm worried?" She wanted to make a joke, but the anxiety in her own voice was clear. She was ready to whine for his cock. Beg for it. Scream.

He pumped against her and sat up so he straddled her waist. Then, he took her hands in his and pinned them to the bed over her head. Her dress had ridden up on her midsection, and his erection lay against her through fine fabric. She'd never wanted a man inside her this much, and he was just sitting there watching her. Denying her.

She bucked up against him, and he had the nerve to laugh. "Get off." He knew she didn't like being teased, yet he did it anyway.

"Is that an order?"

Again, she tried to throw him off with her hips, but he was too heavy. "You'll never get off again when I'm done with you."

"Shhhhh." He released one of her hands and rubbed down her side. She ought to have clawed at him, but didn't. "I just want to look at you. You know that gets me just as hot as when your hot cunt turns to honey all over my face, don't you?"

He undid his belt with one hand, and didn't brush her away when she helped this time. When his erection was out of his trousers, she licked her lips.

In that moment, she wanted nothing more than for him to press his cock inside her mouth and ride her face until she couldn't think about anything else but trying not to choke on it. She wanted him to overwhelm her senses as much as he'd overwhelmed her emotions.

But he ignored her obvious invitation. "It's embarrassing." He fisted his cock and squeezed, not seeming embarrassed at all. "I could come in my pants watching you dance. When you're teasing all those fucks at a bar as Carmen, I lose my fucking mind. I have to press down on my fly to keep from embarrassing myself."

She licked her lips again. "Then don't watch."

He released his cock and held her jaw. His thumb probed her lips and she ran her tongue across it. It tasted salty, like him.

"Don't you get it? I can't *not* watch."

She didn't want him bringing all of these confusing emotions in here—in what she'd started thinking of as their bedroom. Right then, she was glad that they'd never fucked in her condo. She'd never be able to sleep there again, after this was over, if he'd done this there. They were still wearing most of their clothes, and yet she felt more naked than she ever had. More open than she'd ever wanted to be.

"Take off your shirt." She needed to get this back to a primal base level. "I want to watch too."

Thank God that he followed instructions. He released her other hand with a meaningful nod that meant not to grab for his cock now that he'd freed her and unbuttoned his fine, white shirt. Every button he revealed his tanned flesh, and a smattering of hair. He was like a Viking, and she truly felt conquered. She could almost picture him removing furs and ravaging a captive.

During one of the dinners that had to stop after this, he'd told her that his father was "super-fucking-Irish," but his mother was Dutch. That must be where he got the height and the barbarian looks from. Even as she loved that she knew that about him, she worried that she would never get all the things about him out of her head. Maybe he'd moved in permanently without her knowing?

When his chest was bare, he leaned down and captured her mouth in a lazy sensual kiss. His hands roamed over her body, over and under her dress. Even though he was so hard against her that it had to be painful, he was in no rush. And even though she could kiss him for hours, she needed him inside her.

"Please, Charlie."

He pulled back and looked at her. His face was so close that she couldn't escape his gaze if she wanted to. If she'd been naked before, when he was holding her down, he was stripping her skin off right now. "What can I give you that you don't already have?"

"Fuck me." His cock twitched against her with the percussive statement, so she knew he was holding back.

"Is that what you want? You just want me to fuck you?"

He knew the truth and she was afraid that he would make her say it. The words *make love to me* were just behind her lips, but she couldn't bring herself to say them. So, she nodded.

"Whatever you want." He reached over and grabbed a condom. She knew she'd fucked up when he slapped her hands away when she tried to help him put it on. "Too fucking turned on for that."

He settled his body over hers, and notched her entrance. Then, he pushed inside her so swiftly it took her breath away. He pushed up on his palms, taking way the friction of his chest against her, and suddenly she felt cold. She was so turned on that she couldn't bear if he stopped, and her hips met his with every thrust.

But something was wrong. He fucked her hard and fast. When she started choking out moans, he pressed her clit hard with one thumb. Usually when they were like this, he whispered to her about how beautiful she was, how much he wanted her. This time, he pulled up her leg until it met her shoulder. It didn't hurt her body when he splayed her wide open and slammed into her. Charlie being rough with her body felt good.

The look on his face, though. She feared that the hardened jaw and the dark gaze wasn't just about how into her he was. There was something distant about the way he fucked her, even as he was deeper inside than anyone ever had been.

The sick part was that the anger may have turned him on even more. The muscles in her thighs began to twitch, heralding another orgasm. This one felt like a big wave from an offshore tropical storm. It was bearing down on her and threatening to choke the life from her.

"Please." She didn't know what she was asking for; she only knew she needed him there with her, and it felt like he'd moved away.

"Are you going to come?" He pressed her clit harder and she squealed as the crest of it hit her. "That's my good girl."

She didn't stop coming, but her eyes snapped open as he lost himself in his own climax. His face twisted into agony as he pressed himself inside her one last time and stayed there. And the misery lingered as his orgasm ended.

Chapter 14

Charlie managed to keep himself from texting Laura for three whole days after their wedding reception. He had a good excuse—the production company needed to prep for a shoot in Chile. They left the morning after *Carmen* opened.

Before the party, he'd been hoping to leave the country as a married man—not just on paper, but for real. That wasn't going to happen now. He knew it in his bones that Laura would never truly open up to him. She would let him do anything he wanted with her body. He could coax a million orgasms from her, but the only way he would ever make her cry was because he made her body feel good.

When he gave in and tapped a few words out on his phone—*Lola invited me over for dinner. Is it okay if I come?*—he felt like a damned chump. He was a beggar for her attention. Even though he'd told himself that he didn't care that she'd left before he woke up the morning after the reception, that it was better that she didn't see him as he was falling apart, it had been like a boulder sitting on his chest to find her side of the bed cold.

She'd wanted to leave so badly that she hadn't woken him up for a ride home. Another motherfucker had seen her in that dress, just fucked and soft like morning. He couldn't fucking stand it.

And it had been all his fault. He didn't know why he had let her see his frustrations the way he had. It was as though he was addicted to her and she was indifferent to him.

The production budget spreadsheets in front of him blurred together. He'd been producing unscripted television for so long that he could set up a budget in his sleep. But, for the past three days, he'd been having trouble concentrating on the most basic tasks.

Maybe he should hit the gym before he headed over to Laura's place. She hadn't responded to his text—he jumped every time his phone lit up—but he had to see her. He'd held out for as long as he could, and he was done.

He just had to make it for another forty-five minutes or so. He could do this.

The next time his phone buzzed, he snatched it up, sure it was a text from Laura. No dice. It was an e-mail notification. The article from *Ocean Drive* was ready, and Phil had agreed to give them a first look after he and Laura agreed to have a photographer at his house. Charlie only had to chase the guy out of the master bedroom once.

He pulled up the article and scanned through. It was mostly about the Miami City Ballet, and he'd nearly waxed poetic about Laura and her dancing. His chest filled with pride. He didn't even try to resist flipping through the pictures.

His wife was gorgeous. She'd worn this red dress, which was almost a longer version of her costume for the show. It skated over her curves like a lover. When he saw himself, he paused. No one looking at that picture would doubt that that man loved that woman. She was inscrutable, but he wore everything in the way he gazed at her, the way he gripped her waist. Just looking at the photos had him remembering the way she'd smelled that day.

He was in love with Laura, and he'd done nothing to stop it. The floor beneath him seemed to give way to new ground. Years and years of trying to become a responsible adult were all wasted because he'd crashed headlong into love with a woman who didn't want him. He'd been crazy to think that they could make a real go of it. Even though his tenacity had given him a very nice life—now in a legitimate business, he couldn't treat his personal life that way.

He couldn't just decide he wanted to be with Laura and have her fall in love with him. Tired of looking at himself mooning over a woman who wouldn't let herself love him back and the orgasms he could give her, he switched back to the article. About three-fourths of the way through, Phil mentioned the tapes and the aftermath. He also had the balls to mention his estrangement from his father. Most articles mentioned the former, but left out the latter. The salacious details always took precedence.

And, in the next paragraph, there was an actual quote from his father:

My son has always gone his own way. We've had our differences, but I'm glad to see that he's turned his life around. Maybe he's more like me than I ever thought—it took the love of his mother to really focus me. Perhaps

*his marriage—settling down—will bring him into the family fold. There's
a spot in New York for him whenever he decides he's ready.*

It was patronizing and awful, his father's specialties, but that's not
what bothered him about the statement. None of it was true. He'd been
focused for years now—on building his production company, keeping a
low profile, feeling like he had something to offer. Laura had nothing to
do with that. If anything, she'd knocked him off his game.

He should be travelling, scouting locations, coming up with concepts
for new shows. He'd felt a modicum of peace when he was on planes and
sleeping in hotels more often than not. This last couple of months with
Laura were anything but settled. He'd been obsessive, jealous, and he'd
smothered her.

But she couldn't travel with him—like Carla and Jonah did. She had a
life here, and maybe in New York someday soon. She might believe that
she'd hit a dead end in her career that it was close to over. But, the way
she'd been dancing lately, there was no way it was true.

The idea of losing her had him wanting to call his father and find out
if that cryptic offer to work for him in New York was true. If it was, he
could just go with Laura. He'd be miserable, not being in charge of his
own life, but he could deal with it if he was with her.

She had years left. And he wanted that for her. But he needed to get back
to being himself. He might not have ever completely fit the image of careless
international playboy, but he had to get his feet back off the ground soon.

Falling deeper into love with Laura would get in the way of that. It
was a blessing that she didn't let him all the way in. Somewhere inside,
he wanted his father's approval. He was man enough to admit that. But, he
wasn't about to give up the life he loved for a woman who didn't want him.

* * * *

Laura's grandfather hadn't said anything when she'd asked him to draw
up divorce papers. Not even when she'd barely been able to get the words
out, and some tears had leaked down her face. Knowing what she knew
now about how his marriage to Lola had ended made her feel a modicum
less of shame about asking for the divorce.

She hadn't thought it would be so hard to do it. After all, she was the
one who'd wanted the annulment in the first place. Wanted to erase even
the idea that they'd ever been married at all. So, it didn't make sense that

she felt as though a knife was plunging through her skin looking at a legal document, one that would end a marriage that had barely even existed.

It didn't help matters that she'd known she was going to have to do this as soon as she left Charlie's house the morning after the reception. As she'd waited on his doorstep in the humid air for a car, she'd had second thoughts. She could have cancelled and crawled back into bed with him. Could have talked about what had happened the night before.

Maybe she should have opened up to him, told him why she was scared to be in love with anyone—much less a man who made her feel like she was on fire in a way nothing had in years.

Instead, she stuck to what she knew—routine, rehearsal, repeat. It felt comforting and awful all at the same time. She could push Charlie out of her mind when she was busy. But, as soon as she stopped, he was right there. And it was just another reason why they couldn't work in the long term.

It wasn't until she read the final version of the article in *Ocean Drive* that she realized the extent of Charlie's success. In just five years, his production company had gone from nothing to supplying six different television networks with original programming.

She'd known that he'd won an Emmy with a cooking show, but she hadn't realized that he wasn't just the money behind that show. He was hands-on with everything he did. The people he worked with practically worshipped him. She'd thought Carla liked him because Jonah liked him. And Jonah liked him because they'd been friends for a very long time. She'd believed that her cousin had overlooked *The Single Guy* and the whole seedy tape thing because of their job. But it wasn't like that. Every time she learned something new about Charlie, she felt shamed by the way she'd treated him after finding out about the marriage.

Even though the decision to end their marriage was the only one that made sense, she wasn't sure she could do it if she just went to him alone. Lola had invited him to dinner. Her grandfather/lawyer would also be there. She was sure her grandmother was thinking it was a double date. But her family were going to be there as a safety valve to make sure she went through with it.

When she had refused to tell Charlie that she wanted more from him than sex, his hurt had shown up in his gaze. It had twisted their wild chemistry together into something almost ugly. And she wouldn't hurt him again and again. In the back of the car leaving his house, when it was too late to turn back and crawl into bed with him, she'd realized the truth—she wasn't just afraid of turning into her empty shell of a mother, she was actually broken. She'd practiced not feeling anything for so long that she had no choice but to reject her connection with Charlie.

If she couldn't tell him how she felt about him, she didn't deserve him.

Lola was making *arepas* for dinner—one of the top five things she shouldn't be eating less than a week before the season started. And she was too nervous to put any food in her stomach anyway. When her grandfather showed up and kissed Lola on the mouth, it was weird. But their relationship or whatever it was grew less weird by the day. Her grandparents seemed happy, and that was all that mattered. Even if they'd tried to destroy each other in the past, they had this easy way around each other that couldn't be denied. They hadn't discussed the fact that he'd cheated on her grandmother. That was mostly because Laura had enough issues with her own crumbling marriage.

Even though she was adjusting to the idea of her grandparents dating each other, she'd exiled herself to the living room to avoid observing any PDA, just to be safe.

When the door chime rang, signaling Charlie's arrival, she jumped off the couch and ran to the door. She should have let Lola answer it because Charlie looked amazing. He was freshly showered, and his hair was still wet. He wore one of his designer suits—the kind that she would have thought were slick and sleazy if they weren't on him. His white shirt showed off his tan, and was unbuttoned enough that she could see his chest hair.

The urge to touch him was overwhelming. She could almost feel the press of his body against hers as she repressed the desire to hug him. Her lips burned from the desire to kiss him. And his gaze seemed to eat her up in the same way she was living again because he was here.

It had only been a few days, but her body craved his like a drug.

She stood, holding the door open, for too damned long. He didn't say anything, and it seemed to her that he was as affected by seeing her again as she was seeing him. It wouldn't make it any easier to tell him that they were going to be over before they planned to be knowing that he still wanted her even though she'd refused to give him what he really needed.

With a great deal of difficulty, she broke his gaze and motioned him inside. "Come in."

He nodded and entered as she moved back. The vestibule of the condo was narrow, and she didn't move back far enough for him not to graze her breast with his arm. Or she could have moved further away, but she was too much of an addict to care.

How had this happened? None of her previous lovers had ever felt this essential before. She'd never been this connected to anyone. Maybe it was because he was exactly the wrong guy for her that she couldn't leave well enough alone.

She wasn't expecting him to lean over and kiss her cheek after she'd closed the door and turned back to him. It was an awkward, chaste thing that made her pulse speed up just the same.

"I'm sorry."

"For what?"

"I didn't want you to leave the other night. Not before we talked."

She hung her head in regret. Couldn't meet his gaze because it would mean that he'd probably see something that gave him hope. "I don't think we have anything to talk about."

His posture stiffened, and he put both hands in his pockets. They stood there for two beats, four. Until Lola stormed in to save them.

"Why are you standing in the doorway?" Lola wore a colorful apron, and her lipstick was only slightly askew. She'd probably paid enough attention to the food that dinner wasn't burnt. "Dinner is ready."

Charlie put his hand on the lower back as she led him into the dining area. They sat on one side of the table, opposite her grandparents. Lola talked about everything and nothing while Laura picked at her food, and Charlie demolished his. It was as though her grandmother sensed that they had so much to say to each other that they couldn't put anything into words.

Or her grandmother was just giddy because she'd fallen in love again. Probably the latter given the number of times she and Charlie got incidentally caught up in the game of footsie played by the septuagenarian couple across from them.

It stabbed Laura in the gut every time one of them got their feet grazed in the sock-laden crossfire. She'd never expected to have that kind of connection with anyone, and it seemed to come out of nowhere. Her parents didn't share looks that said more than a thousand texts. They didn't have their own intimacies. But she and Charlie were starting to have that.

And it was better if it stopped now than when he asked her to give up dancing to follow him around the world. It had to be tonight so that she wouldn't be tempted to call him on the phone when he was travelling next, just to hear him talk about his day.

When everyone—except for Laura—finished their food, she and Charlie got up to clear the table.

"Were you not hungry?" Charlie asked as she scraped her food into the trash.

"I want a divorce." The plate he was holding dropped into the sink with a clatter, and shattered a wineglass. When he went to grab the dish, she pulled on his arm. "You'll cut yourself."

He rounded on her, and she expected to see something in his gaze other than resignation, but that was the only thing there. "Why do you care?"

Couldn't he see that she was doing this *because* she cared about him? She wanted him to have the kind of life that he wanted, and she wanted him to find the sort of woman who could give him that life. It wasn't her, and she would not ever allow herself to be that kind of woman. She couldn't give up everything that made her separate from her mom—ballet—to follow Charlie around the world.

"I do care about you, Charlie."

He ripped his hand away from her, and it felt like more of a loss than it should have been. "Funny way of showing it."

"You don't want me." She wrapped her arms around her waist, afraid to look at him for fear that she would take it all back despite this being the best thing for both of them.

She'd apparently said the wrong thing because he backed her up against the counter, crowding her, filling her nose with his scent and her visual field with his body.

"Did it feel like I didn't want you three nights ago?" He pressed his lower body against hers, and she could have groaned at how he was still half-hard and ready. "Does it feel like I don't want you now?"

She couldn't give in to him. One moment, she'd felt the strength of her convictions, and she'd been ready to end this before either of them really got hurt. Now, she wanted to wrap her legs around his waist and ride him to the kitchen floor. The only reason she didn't was because they weren't alone.

This was how powerful his hold was over her, and this was exactly why getting any more involved with him could destroy them both. She was dangerously close to falling in love with him. She might already be more than halfway there.

He grabbed the sides of her face, and lowered his mouth to hers. The way his gaze had pierced her a moment ago, she would have expected him to ravage her mouth, leaving her lips bruised and searing her skin to his. Instead, it felt as though he was drinking her in. Like he was saying goodbye with his mouth.

Maybe he was having as much trouble with words as she was, but his lips against hers were a benediction. Their tongues dancing, the grip of his hands on her hips, how tightly she grasped his shoulders. It was all so desperate, sad and moving that she wasn't surprised when tears slipped down her cheeks. He must have tasted them because he deepened the kiss for a moment, and she could barely stifle a sob into his mouth.

He was killing her without even trying. People had already been hurt—maybe her even more than him. She wanted him, and couldn't have him leave doubting exactly how much. He was breath and light and hope.

And she was throwing it all away for a career. What kind of fool did that make her?

Abruptly, too abruptly, he pulled away and grabbed a pair of kitchen tongs. She found a plastic bag under the sink and cleaned up the broken wineglass in silence. It took a long time, way too long.

This simple domestic task, probably being performed across the world by different couples felt heavy and meaningful. Every time he brushed against her or she him, sparks that felt like home skipped across her skin.

Every time he moved away, she tried to remind herself that hope was what got her caught up in something she couldn't control. Hope and tequila.

Chapter 15

"The shoot will take fourteen days, but you guys only have to be down for seven." Jonah looked relieved, and Carla appeared to be disappointed at the short shoot. "I'm going to go down with a camera man and wrap up all the background footage, do all the set up myself."

"Laura's not going with you?" Now, Carla seemed to be confused.

Charlie shook his head. "No, she and I aren't—we're not together."

Technically, they were still married. The day after the dinner at her condo, a messenger had showed up at his house with divorce papers. She'd been planning it all along—probably since the first time they'd fucked. He couldn't help the tendrils of betrayal that wound their way through his gut thinking that all the time they'd spent together, even after he'd offered her something real instead of a charade for the press, had meant nothing.

Despite her protestations of having feelings for him, she was just as cold as he'd feared. Why did he always have to offer his love to people who didn't believe he was good enough? It was whiny and self-indulgent to wonder, but it was true.

He'd started a production company so that he could prove to his father that he was just as capable as his brothers. And the only time the man had ever said anything nice about him was when there were cameras on or reporters about.

He'd offered Laura a real marriage based on more than just chemistry. He was in love with her passion for dance, and he'd thought she could see that being with him wouldn't take that away. She believed that he would be the end of something she'd loved her whole life, not the beginning of something new and exciting.

He'd been willing to eat his own pride and work for his father if he could be with her. And she wasn't willing to give him anything in return. The thought left him feeling hollow inside.

He must have drifted off and missed part of the conversation because Jonah put his giant hand on his shoulder and said, "You okay, man?"

Charlie shrugged him off, and took a beat to ponder whether to be honest with his friend. He and Jonah had known each other since college. Charlie had been a rich, entitled fuck. And Jonah had been the scholarship football player from a tiny town on one of the smaller islands of Hawaii. His friend had been overwhelmed by the spotlight of playing football for one of the premier programs in the premier conference in the country. Somehow, Charlie had decided that he would be a good guide.

They were an odd couple, for sure. But they had never lied to one another. When Jonah had dropped out following his girlfriend's suicide and the media shit storm that had followed, Charlie had told his friend that it was a terrible idea—that he was throwing away his life. Then, he'd ordered Jonah the most expensive camera he could fit on his emergency credit card and had it delivered to Jonah's house. Charlie had remembered Jonah loving a photography class sophomore year, and he at least wanted him to have something to do while he figured out his life.

And then Jonah had become a Pulitzer Prize-winning photographer.

"I'm not doing so hot, buddy."

Carla narrowed her gaze, and he regretted opening up until Jonah said, "I gotta talk this out with Charlie, princess. You mind?"

His wife communicated something silently in a way that felt like a stab wound to Charlie. He and Laura would never have that, and at this point, she was the only person he could imagine feeling that way about.

Jonah turned his chair, so he was facing Charlie, who kept his body turned to the conference table. His friend might look like boulders of muscle piled on top of bones that could crush concrete, but he was a deeply sensitive and perceptive man. That was how he'd become a wildly successful photojournalist before meeting Carla.

"How soon after you met Carla did you know she was yours?"

Jonah leaned back and scrubbed his hand down his face until he landed in a thoughtful beard stroke. "You're in love with her, aren't you?"

"Am I that fucking obvious?" He faced his friend, then. And immediately got annoyed with the wry grin on his face.

"No, but I've just known you too long." He shook his head. "And I can never remember you getting depressed over anything—much less a girl."

"You didn't see me after that tape got released." But even that, when he should have been at his lowest, hadn't felt like this. Back then he'd been motivated by the negative attention from his father and the media. He'd set out to prove everyone wrong about him and he hadn't put his head back up until he'd accomplished that. "This is different. Laura is different."

Christ, he didn't even like saying her name out loud, as though uttering the words would drain more of her essence from him. He felt like he was losing her a little bit more every time he said it.

"I knew that Carla was mine when she told me she was having my baby."

"Laura was mine the second she said her vows, even though neither of us really remember them." He put his forehead on the table, the glass fogging with his breath. "I didn't know it yet. She didn't. But, I've never been with someone who fits me that well before."

"I had to prove to Carla that I was ready, too. She wanted to push me away—was just going to introduce me to her family and put up deuces."

"She was going to raise Layla alone?" The idea of Jonah not getting to be a father to Layla hurt Charlie. He might just be an unofficial uncle, but the way Jonah and Carla loved their baby girl—the way she fed their love for each other—was beautiful. The idea that they'd almost lost that was wounding.

"I think she loved me, too. But I had to show up for her."

"Laura wants me to go away. She served divorce papers."

"The last time you saw her, did it feel like it was over?"

The last time he saw Laura narrowed down in his mind to that kiss in her kitchen. The way she'd touched him, the taste of her salty tears in his mouth. No, it hadn't felt over. Even though their words had said differently.

"No, but I don't want to stalk her creepily until she gives in. Maybe I need her to come to me?"

"No." Jonah's booming voice could have shaken the window panes if they weren't made of thick, tempered glass. "That's the last thing you need to do. I shouldn't be telling you this because Carla wouldn't touch my dick anymore if she found out, but you have to know that Laura's family is fucked up, right?"

"Yeah." While her parents hadn't done anything overtly awful after their initial meeting, he caught something haunted in Laura's gaze whenever they were mentioned—especially her mother.

"Laura's mom has a drug problem that no one talks about." Jonah's words shocked the shit out of Charlie. "Apparently, she stays high because Mr. Delgado is a dick to her."

"Why doesn't she leave him?" Laura would certainly support her mother if she sought any sort of help. He didn't know everything about his wife—not as much as he should know—but he knew that for sure.

"She was fucked up by how her mother refused to leave Cuba with the rest of the family. Then, she fell in with her douche husband, and refuses to hear talk about leaving him."

"But how does this relate to me and Laura?"

"This is the part that Carla's going to castrate me over." Charlie motioned him to keep talking. He needed to hear all the good stuff. "Laura has always said that she'll never get married. She doesn't want to end up unhappy and catatonic like her mother. As soon as she could get out of that house—she was fourteen when she moved in to the ballet academy, and she travelled to dance camps every summer—she got out."

"And she never looked back." It was so much to think about. Getting married to him had ripped open wounds that she'd been running from for decades. Loving him wouldn't just mean giving up her ballet career, it would mean giving up who she'd thought she was forever. Could he ask her to do that? Knowing it might make her crumble? Could he walk away from her, even if that's what she needed?

"I'd say she looked back when she hooked up with you."

"That was a drunken mistake."

Jonah shrugged on of his massive shoulders again. "You know what they say about '*in vino veritas*.'"

"But how do I show her that being with me doesn't mean that she has to give up anything?" Charlie wanted her to have everything she wanted. Everything.

"What means the most to her?"

"Ballet." Even given all the revelations dropped today, he knew that for a fact. She might be a little tired, but dance was the only thing she'd ever allowed herself to be passionate about.

"You have to show her that she can have you *and* ballet. Together, at the same time."

Charlie could do that. He would show that she didn't have to give anything up to have him. He would show her that being together made the dancing more—that he could make her life easier. He'd keep her more insulated from her family bullshit than locking herself away in a rehearsal studio ever had.

And sure, he wanted kids and a home base. He wanted all of it. But he could wait for his. As long as Laura was there at the end of the wait.

Chapter 16

Laura felt as though she was flying across the stage. Her body hadn't felt this light in ages. Her movements were perfectly timed with the music, and she could *feel* the audience leaning in to every gesture.

She was dancing, center stage, inside a ring of male dancers in chairs. During this piece of the show, she was playing at seducing them. But this didn't feel like play. She could almost see Charlie sitting in one of the chairs, looking at her like had on the wedding video. He'd been a little in awe of her when she'd approached him at the bar. He hadn't been able to fake it.

The only way she'd gotten through the remainder of rehearsals had been thinking about Charlie. He was going to be at the front of her mind, regardless. So, she used that as fuel. If she'd stopped to ponder the fact that he was gone from her life, even for a moment, she would have broken into a million pieces. She would not have been able to get off the floor, much less leap.

The whole theater held its breath on the final set of turns before the end of her solo. Her leg cut through the air as the music crescendoed, and her body filled with the joy and longing of the character she played.

As she stopped in a plié, her arm and gaze extended up to the ceiling, the stage lights hit her eyes. That had to be the explanation for the tears threatening to send her mascara and fake eyelashes down her face.

She managed to fight the tears until the end of the show. She took her bows, and rushed to her dressing room. Although she made it there in one piece, the bouquet of roses she'd been holding didn't fare so well. She'd beheaded them against a sharp corner in her haste.

Tossing the stems on the couch, she made her way to the stool at the counter. The lighted mirror was helpful in applying makeup and making sure costumes were perfect, but she couldn't look herself in the face right now. She was afraid that the woman looking back at her wouldn't really be the her she wanted to be anymore. Her insides were rending themselves at the pull between the life she'd always wanted, the life she was living tonight, and the man who'd set her heart aflame in just a few short weeks.

Her whole body buzzed when someone knocked at the door. Hoping it was Charlie despite herself, she hopped up and opened it to a stranger.

He must have recognized the shock on her face because he extended a hand. "I hope I'm not disturbing you."

"No, you're not."

"Gil Rosen, I'm with the New York City Ballet."

"Oh?" She motioned him inside the dressing room, keeping the door open. She recognized the name, and his face was familiar now that she could place it.

"Yes. I'm on vacation with my husband, but I can't seem to leave work behind." He pulled up the legs of his well-tailored pants and sat on the edge of the couch. "Matthieu called me and told me I needed to see your performance, and he wasn't wrong."

She waited for the excitement to bubble up at the possibility he was here to offer her something. And waited. And waited.

Two years ago, she would have given her eye teeth for an opportunity with the New York City Ballet. If this had happened before her injury, she would have barely been able to contain herself.

But now? All she felt was resignation. He was probably just here out of a courtesy to Matthieu, to compliment her on her performance, but even the possibility that he was going to offer her something that would take her away from Charlie was too much.

"We'd been planning to do *Carmen* next season."

Laura sat on the stool. "With Matthieu's new choreography?"

"Yes. And some performers from the Met are interested in participating."

That made total sense.

"Who were you thinking of having dance the lead role?"

"You."

Excitement and fear mixed with the nothing in her stomach to make nausea. With the reason for his visit on the table, her foreboding should have dissipated. The universe was showing her that she'd made the right choice. If that was the case, why did she feel a blanket of sadness settling over her.

"You're not interested?" Gil's gaze narrowed. Her lack of excitement must have shown up on her face.

She pulled herself together and nodded vigorously, shaking the tears out of her eyes. "Absolutely. I'm just so surprised. This has been a lifelong dream."

"You'd be a guest performer for this piece." Gil's posture softened, as though he was relieved she had said yes. Her entire career as a dancer, she'd been at the mercy of company directors, choreographers, teachers who needed to say "yes" for her to succeed. This was the first time in her career that someone had come to her needing something from her in order to make something work. For someone who had always been fungible, it was a heady experience. That sensation cut through her sorrow about leaving Miami. After all, she'd never had a problem leaving her family before. They weren't even here tonight, and they usually made all of her openings. She knew it was because it would look bad if they didn't, but it still meant something to her.

"I understand, and I would be delighted to join you."

"And if you're interested in joining the company, this would be an excellent audition."

"It's been my dream forever, Mr. Rosen."

* * * *

Laura was talking to another man. Pretty much the only man who could take her from him successfully.

Charlie heard enough to get the gist of the conversation from outside her dressing room. Laura had been invited to dance for the New York City Ballet. In the role she'd just danced so beautifully that Charlie could scarcely believe it was his woman on stage instead of some sort of goddess of dance.

He'd shown up with signed divorce papers, a bouquet of flowers, and a bottle of tequila. Symbols of leaving the past behind, a tribute to her gorgeous dancing, and a way to toast the future—their future.

The plan had been to tell her that he wanted to start over and date, that it had been a terrible idea to do that while they were still married. He'd wanted the chance to show her, over a long period of time, that they were right for each other.

The instant he heard her agreeing to leave Miami temporarily, in the hopes of leaving for good, he knew he'd made a mistake. He thought about leaving without talking to her. He didn't know if he could be decent about this right now. When she'd talked about moving to New York, it had been a distant possibility. Now that it was right here, he couldn't wrap his head around it.

Everything he'd told himself about how he would cope—working for his father and moving with her—fell away.

He couldn't do that, and he wouldn't be a man who deserved Laura if he did. So, he shouldn't see her right now. Like a wounded animal, he might lash out. And he wouldn't—couldn't—allow her to bear the brunt of it.

She'd chosen the ballet, and herself. He couldn't actually blame her for that. All her life, she'd had to rely on only one person—the one in the mirror. It would be unfair for her to expect him to be there for her. It would be insane for him to expect her to rely on his love for her. He hadn't even told her about that. But it was there. It was the fact that he'd married her in the first place.

He'd been in love with her even then. His chest felt tight, and breathing felt like choking.

If it had merely been a lust thing, they would have hooked up at the wedding. She wouldn't have snuck away in the morning, and they would have had lazy, hung-over sex. Maybe it would have been awkward when they saw each other again, but he would have been able to stay away.

He wouldn't have sponsored her ballet in hopes of spending more time with her. Wouldn't have threatened a reporter for saying words about her.

If he hadn't been in love with her, he wouldn't have made her go to dinner with him to sign those annulment papers. Even if his subconscious hadn't made him marry her, he wouldn't have felt the driving need to touch her again even now.

Moments from making his escape and faxing the damned papers to her house, he must have caught her eye.

"Charlie." She sounded surprised to see him. As surprised as he was to still be standing outside her dressing room like a rube.

He shook off his black mood and decided to pretend that he hadn't just had his heart ripped out. Instead of tossing the divorce papers at her, throwing the flowers in the trash, and taking the bottle of tequila to the beach so he could get drunk and drown himself in the ocean, he walked in and shook the man's hand.

"Gil Rosen."

"Charlie Laughlin."

"Oh, the husband?"

Laura slid her hand in the crook of his arm. She might as well have stuck a knife in his back. It was all for show. Every bit of affection she'd given him had always been for show.

"Yes."

The other man didn't see his wince because he turned his attention on Laura. "You'll share the good news?" The guy's wink was like a gunshot. Charlie felt like crumpling to the floor and dying. He'd clearly spent too much time around ballet people. All the drama and longing had made him go soft.

"He'll be so excited for me." She rubbed his arm, and it was all he could do not to slap her away. "He knows that I've been wanting this for so long."

When Gil walked out of the room, he yanked his arm away from Laura. Not even looking her in the eye, he tossed the divorce papers on the counter. "They're signed."

She approached him from behind and put a hand on the middle of his back. "Don't."

"Don't what, Laura?"

"How much did you hear?"

"I heard enough to know that you're leaving."

He thought he heard a sob on her voice, but he wouldn't turn to look, before she said, "I have to go."

"I know."

"You deserve someone who can give you what you want."

She still didn't understand. The things he'd said before he'd realized that Laura was his person didn't matter. He didn't need kids or a white picket fence kind of boring life. *He needed her.*

Finally, he turned. Her gaze was all fractured, black glass. She hated this as much as he did. But she had her war paint on. The costume, the severe bun, the heavy makeup—he longed to rip it all off and touch the woman underneath.

His cock didn't care that she was ruining both of their lives. Whenever she went near him, he needed to be inside of her. He wanted to rain kisses all over her face, down her neck, down to the very core of her where he knew he could make her come apart until her will to leave him was so weak that she would promise to stay with him for another orgasm on his tongue.

The desire to bite her neck, to mark the perfect skin where her shoulder met her graceful neck pulsed through him.

She must have felt his energy change because she backed up. "This isn't a good idea."

"What isn't?"

"This is not how we solve this problem." She brought her hands up. He took another step forward, and her palms met his chest.

Chapter 17

"What problem?" Charlie knew he was pushing it with her. Her need to get away from him was palpable. That didn't stop him; it just made him want his wife even more.

"I'm leaving, Charlie." She motioned to the cursed manila envelope on the counter. "If we have sex now, we'll just confuse things."

Charlie shook his head. "I'm not confused."

He grabbed her wrist, gently enough that she could pull away if she tried at all. Then he dragged her hand down his body, gratified to see her pulse increase speed at her neck. When he pressed her hand against his cock, she cupped him. It was excruciating. From the flush of her neck, she was on the edge herself.

Close to coming, he grabbed both of her hands and wrapped her arms around his neck. Her body flush with his shifted and moved. He was about to embarrass himself just from standing there in front of him.

"I'm not confused when your fuck-hot little body squeezes my cock while I'm riding it."

She bucked against him, but he wasn't going to let her go until she heard him out. "I'm not confused about being the one who makes sure you eat something before I get my dessert."

She stopped moving, relaxing into his embrace. "We shouldn't."

"I want to say goodbye to my wife." He lowered his head so his mouth was close to her ear. Even sweaty from exertion, the scent of her made him mad. "Are you going to give me that?"

She glanced towards the closed door. "Here?"

"If I let you go, you're not going to let me have it."

"It?"

"That thing that I only feel when I'm with you." He maneuvered both their bodies to the door so he could flip the lock. Even in a small room, he knew he would lose her if he stopped touching her. If she couldn't feel how hard she made him for a split second, she would deny them both.

And he needed to give her one last, good fucking before he bid her goodbye. He needed to take his time with her, getting her off before he could let her leave him for good.

He wanted to make sure that she couldn't get off with any of the motherfuckers who would try to get in her pants once they found out she didn't belong to him anymore. Needed to be imprinted on her mind and her body forever.

He'd moved them over to the couch, the one where he had made her come with his mouth. At first, he wasn't sure what he wanted to do with her. The only guidance his brain gave him was a primitive chant of: *take, plunder, fuck.*

"You want this, don't you?" Instead of listening to the caveman part of his brain, he was able to use his words. He searched her face for any sign of hesitation. All he found there was her lust-darkened gaze, and a stain on her cheeks that he didn't think was entirely the result of stage makeup.

"I do." Her words were too close to wedding vows, too earnestly spoken.

Instead of responding, he kissed her and pressed her down to the couch. He licked inside her mouth, ate her moans as he flexed his hips against her open legs. Within moments, they were dry humping like teenagers, and he was close to coming. The only thing that stopped him from letting himself do that was the thought that this was the last time he'd be with her.

When he pulled back, her bun was askew, and her lipstick was smeared across her face. Her costume remained in place, but he intended to change that. He thought about ripping the thing off of her. After all, part of his money had paid for it. But he didn't want to do that. Needed to slow down and savor her.

"Sit up."

She followed his instructions, and it satisfied that part of him that became feral with this woman. His fingertips brushed down her spine as he unzipped the red fluttery thing that she'd seduced the entire crowd with. Obediently, she lifted her hips so he could pull off the dress and the tights she wore underneath. Once he got to the ribbons on her toe shoes, he let himself rip. She gasped.

"I'll buy you new ones." He winked at her. "Consider it alimony."

When she was finally naked, he let himself look at her. Lithe and graceful everywhere. Her feet bruised, battered, and ugly in a beautiful way. He cupped her high arched feet, and spread her muscled legs. Even though she could probably crush bones between her thighs, she melted like butter for him.

She cried out when he finally let himself touch her clit. He'd slept with a respectable number of woman, but none of them had ever responded to him like this. He'd spent enough time with Laura to know when she was faking something with dance. She never faked anything when they were together.

"You can't pretend with me, gorgeous." He pushed one finger inside her and let her squeeze him inside of her. "I know you'll miss this."

She didn't respond because he pressed his thumb to her clit on every stroke. And he went slowly, so slowly. He knew she'd probably start complaining about his pace soon. But, if she was only going to give him a few stolen minutes before telling him to get lost, he was going to take every damned one of those minutes.

The minutes weren't damned—they were blessed and sacred. It was he who was damned to love a woman that he couldn't hold onto. He wanted to punish her for leaving him by giving her so much pleasure that she forgot why she had to go.

He let her get close to coming—hips pumping, creeping flush on all of her naked curves—and then he withdrew his fingers, licking them clean. Right then he decided that he wouldn't give her his mouth. That part was to punish himself. He wanted to remember the night of their wedding reception as the last time he had that. On his knees for this woman who couldn't love him back.

He crawled up the couch until he straddled her waist.

"What are you doing?" She pressed her hips up against him; his aching cock protested fiercely.

But he had a mission. He started pulling bobby pins out of her hair. He needed to bury his hands in it almost as much as he needed to bury his cock inside her. There was something different about her when her hair was down and wild. She was beautiful when she was all gussied up for a performance, when she was dancing and far away on a stage, but he needed the real, close-up Laura. He wanted her to be just as wild and primitive as his desire for her.

"You're wasting time." She sounded irritated, but he didn't look down at her face, just concentrated on his task. Already, she was turning from the woman he loved into the woman he'd torture himself to be with. He could even see months and years down the road that thinking about her irritated voice and the way she lifted her chin that said *I'm too good for this shit*, would make him have to stroke himself off. "Are you going to fuck me or style my hair?"

He actually growled at her. Like an angry bear. She'd wounded him fatally, and now she wanted him to rush his death scene? He couldn't do that, wouldn't even try. "I'm going to fuck you." He pulled out the last pin, and wrapped her ponytail around his fist. He moved her head so their gazes met, but he was above her. "But you're not going to rush me, gorgeous."

He felt a shiver move through her body, as though she was both frightened of the way she was affecting him and exhilarated by having him manhandle her. He shouldn't have acted this way. Should have been on his knees and indulging them both in the way she moved over his face. She should be crying out again and again. And then he should be slipping out of the room.

Maybe it was because this time was different. This was a farewell that neither of them wanted. But she was too afraid to fight for them. And he had too much pride to beg her to stay, knowing that she'd leave him in the end regardless.

"Do you want my cock or not?"

"I—I want it." He loved it when her voice got all shaky.

"Then you're going to take it on my terms?"

* * * *

Laura didn't know the man on top of her. It couldn't be the one she'd married. None of that sunny, laid-back dude was left. That man who she craved had maybe never entered the building tonight. Instead, she was at the mercy of a barbarian who looked like Charlie Laughlin, even sounded like him, but there was something fundamentally changed about him.

And she fucking loved it.

Maybe everything Charlie did to her she would like? Maybe there was something wrong with her that the feel of his hand against her scalp and the prickle of pain she felt every time she tried to move her head on her own power made her so wet that she could feel the arousal dripping down her thighs.

She'd never been into the seemingly cold dominant thing, but that wasn't this. His breath was labored, as though he'd been running. But no, he was just holding her down. There was emotional weight here. When his finger had been inside her, when he'd ripped that orgasm away and licked her off his hand with a mean look on his face, she realized that she'd caused this.

In that moment, she'd wanted to lay herself out like his sacrificial lamb. Needed to be both the sacred and the profane for him. The wife and whore.

If he needed to use her like a fuck doll in order to let her go, she wouldn't just bear it. She'd fucking love it and never be able to come again without thinking of his long fingers strung through her hair or playing with her pussy.

He kissed her again and she tasted her arousal in his mouth. She felt too naked and exposed to him and worked the buttons on his dress shirt. She wished she'd thought ahead and stolen one of them to take with her. She knew she wouldn't get the opportunity to do so again. He'd given her all the time and attention that he was willing to give, and she'd have to live with that.

This sure-to-be angry fuck was going to kill both of them. And it was going to be the headstone on their fucked-up failed marriage. One of his buttons got stuck and her sob of frustration ended up in his mouth. He pulled back, and pushed her fingers away.

Instead of removing his shirt, he grabbed her hair again and turned her around, so she was facing the back of the couch, the wall. He was going to deny her the opportunity to look at him.

"I need to look at you." Her whisper was ragged and wanton. She felt pathetic begging him, but she needed to see the man who almost made her give up everything when he pounded into her.

"You want my cock, and I'm going to give it to you how I want to." He punctuated the statement with a hard slap on her ass.

The shock of it made her pull at his grip, which didn't fail. The impact didn't turn her off, though. She needed him even if he was going to take her like a stranger.

It hadn't felt like this the first time. She missed his worshipful touch from that first night they'd spent together. But maybe it was better that he was ending it like this.

"Is anyone still backstage?" His question caught her off guard.

"The crew, maybe." She didn't know how long she'd been back here between the adrenaline of the show, the job offer, and Charlie— always Charlie.

"Then bite down on the cushion." She didn't know what he meant until she heard the sound of paper ripping, and felt his sheathed cock at her entrance. "So fucking wet for me, wife. You may not want me anymore, but this pussy needs me. What are you going to do when you move away from me? Are you going to stroke it yourself?"

She bit down on the cushion to stop herself from saying yes.

"Gonna try to replace me?"

He entered her and she screamed, and when he didn't move, she tried to push her hips back into him. She needed him to move. To fuck. To take her like he'd promised with every touch that came before this.

"Don't move." He pumped his hips a little, but not enough. Then, he stroked down her spine and spread her ass cheeks. "I want to see where I'm seated so far in my wife that I made her scream."

She shook her head, but released her bite on the cushions to say, "Yes. Yes."

As though that gave him permission, he started moving again. With every drag of his cock against and inside her most sensitive flesh, she saw stars. His animal grunts, which would have taken her completely out of the moment with anyone else, turned her inside out until her movements were shaky and writhing.

He pulled her on and off of him by the hair, which burned and ached. It made her feel used, and she hated that she loved it. She hated that she loved him, and she'd turned him into a rutting animal. Even if her body loved it, her heart was breaking.

All of her guilty conscience, the only thing that was keeping her from coming apart, fled when he reached around the front of her body and rubbed her clit. She couldn't think. And, even though, she couldn't see him with her vision, she could picture his face—all of his expressions. Sacred. Profane. Love and hate all mixed up.

Again, he took his finger away right before she came. He pulled her up so she was flush with his still clothed body, which made her feel even more cheap and used.

"Hold the back of the couch."

Even though she shouldn't want this degradation, she followed instructions. Her knuckles went white when he slammed inside her again. After another brief rub on her clit, he had her over the back of couch. Her clit rubbed against the upholstery with every stroke. She would have frozen when he touched her back entrance with his thumb had she not been so close to coming that her back teeth were grinding together.

Instead of saying a word, making him stop, she canted her hips back and gave him permission. She wanted him to overwhelm her, take her over completely. She needed him to punish her body. But she didn't expect it to feel good. And it felt so different, so dark, but still so much pleasure all at once broke her.

She bucked and screamed, and if anyone was in the hall, they certainly heard her. But she didn't care. Not when he slammed inside her for the last time. Not when she wished there hadn't been barriers between them. Not when she wanted to take it all back and stay married to him.

Chapter 18

Charlie knew the day that Laura left Miami, probably for good. Not only did Carla tell him point blank that he was a stupid idiot for letting her walk out on their marriage, but he had felt it in his bones that she was really gone before his best friend's wife plopped down in the chair opposite his desk.

"This is bad." She said nothing else, just leaned back and crossed her arms over her chest.

Charlie looked back down at the spreadsheet he'd been staring at for the last five minutes. "What's bad?" When she didn't respond when he continued, he said, "I'm your boss, you know."

"You're really more of a business partner."

She had a point. Both she and Jonah had a stake in the show and were credited as executive producers.

"Are you going to tell me why you're being awkward, or am I going to have to guess?" Charlie only flirted with Carla in front of Jonah, because it pissed him off. When they were alone, they felt more like siblings.

"You look like you've been sleeping on a bed of nails for about a month." She squinted at him. "Sort of lackadaisical and constipated."

He sniffed, although she had the lackadaisical part right. "How does one appear constipated?"

"Using that form of a verb doesn't help."

"Do you have a point?" He threw his pen across the desk. It ricocheted off the edge and slid across the floor.

Carla seemed to light up at his expression of exasperation. "You're totally brokenhearted."

"And your point?" There was nothing he could do about the fact that Laura left him. All he could do now was regret the way he'd said goodbye.

After he'd regained consciousness and the ability to use his limbs, neither of them had said a word. He tucked his used-up cock back into his pants and walked out. He'd swiped the tequila, and called a car. By the time he'd gotten to his house, he'd been too drunk to use a phone. If he'd been any more cogent, he would not have been able to resist calling Laura and begging her to give him another chance.

She would have turned him down, as well she should have.

"That this is bad."

"I don't see how talking about it is going to make it any better."

Carla stood up and leaned over his desk. "I think that you need to go to New York."

"I can't." He did need to get out of Miami, but he needed to get further from his soon-to-be ex-wife, not closer. "I'm flying to Chile tomorrow."

"You shouldn't go." She straightened up and crossed her arms. "In fact, I'm forbidding you to go."

"Even if I admit that you and Jonah are partners, that doesn't mean you can tell me what to do."

She shrugged. "I tell everyone what to do. That's sort of my thing."

"Can you go somewhere and boss Jonah around right now?" He scrubbed his hands over his tired face. "I just, I don't need this right now. Us breaking up was the best thing for everyone."

"Then why do you look like someone held you down and made you watch them drown a kitten?"

"That's a little graphic. It's not that bad."

"It is." She sat back down, and all hope of getting rid of her fled. "Laura's mother went to rehab the night of the opening. That's why they weren't there."

"I don't see what that has to do with me." Laura was gone, and if he couldn't have gotten her to stay, he was sure her mother's stint in rehab wasn't going to change things.

"I think it has *everything* to do with you."

"Are you going to leave if I don't let you explain?"

"Not a chance." One shake of her red locks, and he knew he'd better settle in.

"Fine." He made a rolling motion with his hand. "Proceed."

"Laura didn't always want to be a ballerina. In fact, we started dance together."

"Don't tell me that you were better." Even though it was none of his business, the urge to protect Laura's reputation remained.

Carla's smile had a devious tone. "No. She was always much better than me. But she didn't really care about dance, didn't talk about leaving home to go to school, until she was eight."

"What happened when she was eight?" Just thinking about what would have made a little kid want to leave home made him sick to his stomach.

"Her mom fell near the pool at their house, broke her ankle, and she got a pain pill prescription."

"Lots of people get pain pills." Suddenly, Charlie remembered how vehement Laura had been about refusing that ibuprofen at his house, and the full extent of the damage Laura's family had done finally sunk in. The mother's vacant expression, the father's half-disgust. Mrs. Delgado was an addict, and it had twisted his wife up inside. "For almost twenty years—"

Carla nodded sagely. "Yep, and Laura was the first one who saw it. She tried to tell her older brothers, who were almost out of the house by then. They did nothing." Carla sighed, and Charlie willed her to say more. "And when she told her father, he slapped her across the face. I was there. It was like something important changed about Laura right then. She'd been my best friend, and I could always count on her. But it was like her light switched off in that moment."

His fist clenched hard, and he wanted to go to her parents' house and kick her father's ass. Even though his father was a dick, he'd never hit any of his sons. "And she turned to dance."

"With a passion that bordered on maniacal. We lost her as soon as she realized that if she told the truth, no one would believe her. She was gone the second she realized that she could count on no one but herself."

"I still don't see what this has to do with me. I tried to show her that she could trust me, that I was there for her." He shook his head to clear the creeping doubts away. "But she didn't believe me."

"Then you didn't see what I saw."

"What was that?" A desperate thread of hope was trying to work its way into the back of his mind. It got as far as his heart before he grabbed on and snapped it so it couldn't wrap around his guts.

"I've never seen her care about someone the way she cares about you." Carla got up and paced. He'd known her long enough to realize that telling her to calm down or sit down when she got worked up was one very good way to get shanked. "She lights up when she looks at you. And she tries not to look at you because she *knows*."

"Knows what, exactly?" He needed his friend, his wife's best friend to say *she knows that she loves you.* But he wasn't going to shake it out of her.

"She wants you like she's never wanted anything. Not ballet. Not her mother to get well. Nothing."

"I have to hear her say it."

"Then you have to go to her."

"But I tried to go to her on opening night, and she wanted to take the job in New York. She wanted to leave me."

"Who says she has to leave you to take a job?" Carla stopped in her tracks. "You can live anywhere. And travel from anywhere."

"But I've made my home here." Even as he uttered the excuse, he knew it was purely weak sauce. His home was with Laura.

"Dumb dumb head." Carla flicked him on the chest, over his heart—reminding him to mind the constant ache there. "Go find her. Figure out the rest later."

"I'll think about it."

"You're going to have some time to think about it."

Carla bit her lip as though she were hiding something. "Oh?"

"Yeah, I'm knocked up again. So, we need to take a hiatus, partner."

He smiled, and his heart lightened. He knew Carla and Jonah wanted more kids, but he thought they might wait. They were moving on with their life, growing their family.

The idea of another baby for his friend made his desire to go get Laura even more acute. He needed to be with her, and he wasn't going to take no for an answer—not as long as there was hope.

The hole in his chest wouldn't heal without her. It was so bad now that he was willing to take any risk to get her back. He needed to hear her story from her mouth, and he would follow her around until she knew that he was a safe person to show her whole heart to. He would keep her safe from the journalists who might follow him around there. He would love her so much that none of them mattered.

* * * *

After the third show that week, Laura sat in an ice bath, holding her phone. They'd done two weeks of shows in Miami, then she and Matthieu had come to New York to rehearse the show with the new company for three weeks.

She wasn't waiting for a call from Charlie. After she left Florida, she'd given up hope on Charlie calling her. No, today her mother was leaving rehab. And she wasn't going home to her father. She was moving into Laura's condo with Lola. The idea made her nervous, as if her mother was dead set on testing her sobriety by moving in with the mother who had abandoned her.

When Laura had brought it up with Lola over the phone, she'd pushed her off. And from the brief conversation she'd had with her mother two weeks ago, it seemed like Lola had spearheaded the effort to support her mom in getting sober. Just thinking about hearing how clear her voice was had tears welling up in Laura's eyes.

The phone buzzed in her hand, and Laura blinked. Her brother Max.

"*Hermanita, como estas?*" Neither of her brothers had ever called her before their mom went to rehab. They'd been avoiding each other for years as much as they'd been avoiding their parents.

And it was stupid. In the last month, she'd felt like she'd gotten her family back. With that progress and dance, she should feel like she'd gotten everything she'd ever wanted.

Except for Charlie.

She rubbed the spot between her eyes, trying to banish him from her head. "Fine, Max. How's Mom?"

"All settled in with Lola."

"How's that going?" Her free hand clenched on the side of the tub. "Lola got all the liquor out of the house? And she promised not to make out with *abuelo* in front of Mom?"

It was as close to addict-proofing the condo as her or either of her siblings could think of.

Max's bark of laughter shocked her, and the water and ice sloshed around. Her toes were pretty much numb, which meant it was time to get out.

"Yeah, they're going to be fine. All making out in the bedroom."

"Somehow, even that's disturbing."

"I think it's kind of nice." Laura wondered about the wistful tone of her brother's voice. Because he was so much older than her, and because she'd never taken the time to get to know him as an adult, she didn't know him well enough to prod more, even if she wanted to. "But the booze is gone. I delivered it to Maya and Javi, just as you asked."

"Thank you." She decided to start repairing their relationship by revealing something of herself. "It's hard not to be there right now."

"Are you kidding? Mom would never want you to give up your lifelong dream to babysit her. She's incredibly proud of you."

"Yeah?" Her mother had never said it out loud. After the pills had started, she hadn't said much about anyone but her father—her obsession.

"We're all proud of you, *hermanita*." This time, it didn't feel so awkward for him to call her "little sister."

"Even Joaquin? I don't think I've ever seen him express an emotion."

Max laughed again and she reveled in how normal their relationship was starting to feel. "Can you blame him? Every time he cried as a little kid, Dad belted him."

Laura knew exactly why. Her older brother was gay, and her father never would have approved of that. He had tried to beat it out of him. Uber-masculine sporty guy Max would have escaped their father's wrath. Joaquin would have borne the brunt of her father's rage.

Laura didn't remember any of that, and it sent a chill down her spine. She only remembered Joaquin as an adult, and the thought of hurting a little kid made her ache inside. She needed a moment.

"Do you have to go?"

She didn't want to get off the phone, but she didn't want to freeze her feet off either. "No, I just need a second."

When she was out of the bath and wrapped in a bathrobe, she sat down on one of the tables in the empty training room with her phone. "I didn't know any of that."

"I'm sorry." Her brother's voice was heavy with sorrow.

"What for?" She used to blame her brothers for bailing as soon as they were eighteen, but given their options, she couldn't exactly blame them. "You did what you had to do to survive."

"We should have believed you."

She toyed with the sash on her robe, searching for the right words. "There's not much either of you could have done."

"I guess you're right, but we could have gotten you out of there."

"I got myself out."

"We should have been there to help."

Hearing that from her brother almost had her losing it. She'd just never asked for their help because the Delgados didn't do that, at least according to their father. Thinking of that fucked up family motto had her thinking about her mom again. And how much it must have crushed her to leave.

"Have either of you talked to Dad?"

When Max answered, it was like a door slamming. "No. He wasn't going to let her go to rehab. And I don't know if I can forgive him for that."

"Aren't we now supposed to be all loving and forgiving?"

"Some things I can't forget." *Jesus*, she needed to get to know her brother more when she went home. Even growing up there, living there her whole life, it was strange to think of Miami as home. She'd always longed for the anonymity and fame promised by New York. Now that she was here, feeling alone and disconnected from everyone she cared about, she longed for her hometown.

And it wasn't just about Charlie, although he was a big part of it. She wished she had said something when he was leaving her dressing room. She wished she had torn up the divorce papers instead of turning them over to her grandfather.

But it was too late to take it all back. He'd let her know that, as soon as a judge signed the decree, they wouldn't be married anymore.

Chapter 19

Charlie stared at Laura's grandfather in disbelief. His hands were numb, and he felt like the guy who had his heart torn out in that Indiana Jones movie. He rubbed the spot where it used to be and fell into the chair that was thankfully behind him.

"She's not my wife?"

Rogelio looked sheepish, as though he'd never lied before in his life. "Even if she had been your wife, you wouldn't have been married after I filed these papers."

"You mean the fake papers dissolving my fake marriage." Saying that his marriage had been fake out loud made it hard to breathe. He bent over and placed his elbows on his knees, just trying to get air.

"It wasn't my idea."

His head popped up. "Not your idea? You committed fraud." Threatening the man with criminal charges was probably not the way to get straight answers from him, but he had limited options here. He felt as though that string of hope that he'd tried to strangle was unraveling all on its own.

He'd come here to convince Laura's grandfather to delay filing the divorce papers. If only he had a little more time—time to do something big to show her that they belonged together—that they could make things work. He'd wanted to be able to tell her that he'd stopped everything.

"Even if it had been real, I represent Laura, not you." The old man shook his head. "I couldn't have halted the proceedings at your request."

"Since it was never real, then I guess that won't be a problem, will it?"

"Well, no."

Charlie put his head between his knees. She was never his, never belonged to him. He hadn't realized until that very moment that he'd built up the idea of a family with Laura inside his head. Unlike the man standing in front of him, his marriage vows, both sets of them, had meant something. They meant that he was sworn to protect his wife from everyone and everything, including himself.

Still, even though he'd resolved to let Laura go, again and again, he'd had that piece of paper saying that they were man and wife in the back of his head. But it had all been a lie. Heat spread over his skin as anger took over his body.

"This was Lola, wasn't it?"

The old man blanched. "No, don't you get mad at her. I went along with it."

"But why?"

He shrugged. "I'm still in love with my wife."

"The one you had a real marriage with, real children?" Charlie stood up and prowled the office, wanting to knock things off shelves and putting his hands deep in his pockets to protect all the framed photos and awards lining the room. "The marriage that ended in divorce and destroyed your daughter?"

Charlie knew it wasn't fair. The man sitting on the other side of the desk had made mistakes. But this particular mistake hadn't been his idea. "I know all that, but Lola thought it was best."

"Since when do you listen to her?" Charlie had heard enough stories to know that listening hadn't ever been Laura's grandfather's strong suit. No wonder her mother had found a carbon copy in her husband. No wonder Laura was so stingy with her heart. No one had ever given her the space to share it before. "She thought *lying* was the answer to Laura's problems?"

"She thought it was a nudge in the right direction." The old man stood up. "I told her that I was worried about Laura, concerned that she would lose herself if she wasn't able to return to the ballet. Then, Lola got this look in her eyes—one I recognized could not be dissuaded. She saw the two of you dancing together at the reception, it was like an avalanche or a rock rolling down a mountain." He made a locomotive motion with his arms. If Charlie weren't so angry, he would have laughed. "I knew I couldn't stop her, so I at least wanted to give her a good cover story."

"Were you ever going to tell her?" Charlie's heart felt like it was breaking all over again, thinking of Laura getting the news he'd just gotten all alone in New York.

No one in her family knew his woman the way he did. They all tried to manipulate her and maneuver her, never asking her about what she really wanted. They didn't see her the way that he did, and he couldn't fucking stand it. Laura Delgado was glorious, and she deserved for the world to see that. Even more, she deserved to have the love of someone—him—who'd seen that from the start.

"Yes. Eventually. I would have had to tell her. It would have been unethical."

"I should really fucking report this to the bar." Charlie stopped, and the old man got even whiter, if that were possible. Laura had told him that his work as a lawyer was important to him, that he hadn't been able to practice in Cuba because he'd been a dissident, and Charlie wanted to threaten something important to him. Even though he was enraged, he wouldn't follow through on his threat because it would upset Laura. "But I'm not going to. I am going to need you to help me get her back, though."

* * * *

Charlie wanted Laura to shine in her final performance with the New York City Ballet because he wanted that for her. And he wanted her to get a permanent place with them. Then, he would stay in New York and convince her to be with him. Or, if she didn't get a spot, he wanted her to come back to Miami and date him. And then—when she was ready—he wanted her to retire and marry him. He needed to make her happy, and tell her she was loved at least a thousand times a day.

Other than that, he would place no demands on her.

He wasn't surprised when her performance was even more transcendent than opening night. She had a confidence she hadn't shown that night, and she glowed. The fact that it hollowed out his insides thinking that maybe she was better off without him didn't rate. He loved her. The only thing he truly needed—regardless of what he wanted—was for her to know that he loved her and would do anything for her to be happy.

He was sitting fifty rows back since he didn't have the same kind of pull in New York, and the show had technically been sold out. It bothered him that he couldn't see her face. He wanted to hold her jaw in his hands and kiss her like he wished he had the last night.

Just seeing her move had him more keyed up than was polite. He shifted in his seat, probably disturbing everyone next to him. She had a different partner for this production, and it seemed that their chemistry was better than it had been with her partner in Miami. The little half-smiles she gave as she played at seducing him—Charlie was greedy for those smiles to belong to him.

He tried to reassure himself that he would be able to get her back. He couldn't live with the uncertainty. But he had to learn to deal with it. Now that he was in the room with her—even far away—it was so much harder to think about walking away if she decided that she didn't want him. Now that he could see her moving in front of him—the artistry and sensuality of her all tangled up—he didn't know if he could keep his promise to himself. He wanted to rush the stage and bundle her away from him.

The show lasted approximately forever and fifteen minutes. As soon as the dancers took their final bows, after the third standing ovation, Charlie made his move. First, he tried bribing the guy guarding the stage door that led to the dancers' dressing rooms.

With a New York accent, the man told him he was "shit out of luck."

His next and only option if he didn't want to camp out at her temporary apartment, was to wait next to the stage door. So that's what he did. The New York air was chillier than he was used to. Living in Miami for more than one winter had thinned his blood so much that he couldn't rightly call himself a Midwesterner anymore. But he would learn to live with the cold if this was where Laura wanted to be.

He pulled up the collar on his wool coat, his breath coming out as puffs of fog. There were a few other people waiting, mostly little girls and their parents, waiting to meet their idols. Most of the parents looked bored, but the little girls buzzed with energy. He was with them.

He tried and failed not to picture a little girl with Laura's dark eyes and his light brown hair, bouncing up and down in anticipation. She'd be obsessed with ballet, and full of energy. She wouldn't be able to help herself and she'd pirouette down the sidewalk in her patent leather shoes.

Charlie wanted that so much. He wanted whatever Laura would give him, and he only hoped it would be more than nothing at all.

The door opened, and he couldn't breathe. When a man he recognized as Laura's partner walked out and shared a romantic hug with the only other single man waiting outside the stage door, he could finally exhale.

Three or four other dancers came out before Laura's dark head appeared in the door. She had her hair down, so he couldn't see her face, but he didn't need to see all of her to recognize her, for his whole body to thrum back to life.

He waited for her to look up, half convinced that she would walk right past him without a second glance. Maybe his time with her had been a dream and he had actually lost his mind.

When she did look up at him, she didn't look happy. He was instantly afraid that he'd made a mistake by coming here. He should have called first, talked to her over the phone, texted her to make sure it was okay to come.

"You're here." She didn't slap him, so that was something, but her face was still neutral. "What are you doing here?"

He hadn't prepared a speech, thinking that he'd be able to tell her everything that he needed to tell her. Instead, silence stretched out between the two of them. But there was still a strong awareness along with the silence. The air was filled with something.

And then she shivered.

He had his coat off and around her too fast for her to say anything. Faster than he could ask whether it was still okay to touch her.

"You don't have to do that."

"I know." But he would freeze his balls off for the chance to touch her, even if it was just embracing her so she stayed warm. "You need a warmer coat."

"I'm fine."

Silence stretched out between them as he stared at her. He wanted to drink her in, especially if she truly didn't want him. This was as close as he would ever get to the heaven of her hands on him again. He inhaled her shampoo, and fought the urge to kiss her and forget talking.

But they needed to talk, and the way to do that was through talking. "Are you hungry?"

"Always trying to feed me." She rolled her eyes. "Are you trying to fatten me up so I can't dance anymore?"

That hit him in the solar plexus. Couldn't she see that she was killing him? That the last thing he wanted was for her to lose out on her dream? "No, but I don't want you keeling over on stage."

"I have food where I'm staying."

On the one hand, he was happy she was inviting him in to her temporary home. On the other, maybe she just didn't want to dump him for good in public.

"Then, let's go."

* * * *

Sweet Jesus, she'd missed the way Charlie smelled. She'd missed the earnest way he always wanted to see to her needs, and the way he touched her as though she was precious made her weak in the knees. And in the heart.

Until she'd had him, she hadn't realized how much her animal body needed to be touched by someone who cared. She was always having people touch her—dance partners, teachers, trainers—but none of that gave her the sensation of being truly cared for.

And she was glad he came to her. She'd considered leaving the show early, but she didn't want to get a bad reputation. If she'd gone to Charlie in Miami, she would have blown her chance on dancing permanently with the NYCB. And if he'd turned her down, she would have been screwed.

They walked the few blocks to her sublet in silence. He held her hand, squeezed it so tight that it would have been painful if she hadn't needed it that way.

She needed Charlie. And that was just the simple truth of it.

Once they got up to the studio she was renting from another dancer, he filled up the whole space. She put his coat on the chair, and walked over to the tiny kitchenette.

"Breakfast for dinner okay?"

"I'm not hungry." She jumped because she hadn't expected him to be so close to her. But it seemed he couldn't even let a few hundred square feet separate them. "But you are."

"I'm not. I just—" She closed the refrigerator, turned, and looked at him, this lethally handsome man who could have been permanently hers. And her heart just broke.

Immediately, he gathered her close, and her broken sobs soaked his undoubtedly expensive shirt. Luckily, she'd wiped off her stage makeup, otherwise it would have been a total loss. She needed to stop crying, but him hugging her almost made it worse. He was supporting her when she was the one who'd rejected him. It made no sense.

Finally, she pulled herself together and put some distance between them. "I'm sorry."

"Why?" He leaned down and looked into her gaze. She felt so much more exposed than she ever had. "I just want to know how I can fix it."

By promising to be her husband again.

"I—I don't know how to fix it."

"Tell me what it is." His grip on her biceps was so steady, so strong that she didn't feel the need to hold back.

"I shouldn't have pushed you away. I should have given us a chance."

"And I should have waited for you to be ready." His voice was so solemn, as though he was the person who'd screwed this all up.

"You didn't screw this up." He moved them to the tiny couch and settled them both. He pulled her into his side as though she hadn't chosen a career over him a month ago. "I screwed it up."

"Well, technically, your grandparents screwed it up."

She sat up so she could look him in the face. "What do you mean?"

His lips twitched as he wiped the remnants of a tear from her cheek. "We're not married."

Had he suffered a blow to the head since she left in Miami? "No, we're divorced."

"I'm divorced, but not from you."

She shook her head to loosen some of the confusion caused by this conversation. Although she'd been working hard and not sleeping much, none of this made sense because of him, not her. "What do you mean?"

"We were never legally married."

"But my grandfather?" She flattened her palm against his chest, needing his heartbeat to ground her. "And my taxes?"

"Lola."

"The officiant?"

"He wasn't in on it." Charlie shrugged. "I managed to track him down through the hotel. Apparently, we just made him dance and do several shots of top shelf tequila. He blessed us for the free booze, but he didn't perform an actual wedding ceremony."

"But why would Lola want us to believe that we were married?" And why would her grandfather go along with it? She couldn't contain the shrieking quality to her voice.

"She thought we'd be great together." It was a flimsy excuse, but it sounded like her grandmother. They may not have known each other long, but the woman was, by turns, mercurial and overbearing. It made sense that she would decide that she and Charlie belonged to each other and scheme to let that happen.

"Wow." She pressed her finger tips to Charlie's smiling mouth, like she needed to touch it to ensure that it was real. "What was she going to do if we had just gone along with it?"

"Convince us to renew our vows and pull in a real priest." He dropped a kiss on her nose. "I thought you needed that."

"I did." She kissed him back on the mouth, expecting him to take it deeper, but he didn't even allow her tongue through his lips. "So, we're not married."

"We're not."

Uncertainty wound its way through her guts. Maybe he was just here to tell her the news. It wasn't the sort of thing that you told someone over the phone. The whole we-were-fake-married was the kind of thing you told your lover face-to-face. And that's what he was, her lover? Or her former lover?

"What are we now?"

"That's kind of what I'm here to figure out."

She'd pushed him away so much that she wanted to hear from him on this issue first. Ever since her mom had gone to rehab, a bandage had been ripped off a festering wound she'd been trying to ignore for years. Her emotions were raw, and her nerves were frayed. But she felt alive to wanting something beyond getting through the next performance for the first time in a long time. She'd felt the first tingles of that with Charlie, but she'd convinced herself that being in a real marriage with him was off limits.

As it turned out, it had been. "What do you want?"

He answered her by pressing his mouth to hers, deeper this time. "I want you," he said against her mouth. Leaving her frustrated again, he pulled away. "I want to date you."

"That feels like a step back." Part of her was afraid that if they were "just dating" it would be easy for her to push him away.

"What do you want us to be?"

She bit her bottom lip, and tried to sort through all the insane thoughts roaming through her brain. He wasn't her husband, but she'd been thinking of him as her spouse for months. That was the truth that felt the most right when she articulated it to herself. Calling him her "boyfriend" or her "lover," even her "partner" didn't sound like who he was to her.

He'd opened the door to something more than her love of dance, and he'd let her walk through it by being himself—patient, kind, caring— everything her father wasn't.

She kissed him again on the mouth, not being able to get enough of his lips against hers after so much time apart. She hoped that kissing him would quiet the doubts she was having about what she wanted to say—what she was dying to ask.

He pulled back when she splayed her fingers inside his shirt, hoping that the feel of his skin might dissuade her from saying the word, asking the equivalent of jumping off a bridge with nothing but a cord of elastic between her and certain death.

And then he did the worst thing; he looked at her. And she saw nothing but love there.

"I want you to be my husband."

His grip on her tightened, but he froze. He hadn't been expecting her to say it. "You want to be my wife?"

It surprised no one more than herself that she wanted to be tied to this man forever. She wanted their names to be said on the same breaths. And she needed him by her side for the rest of her career—and after. Loving him made her stronger, not weaker. He was not a perfect man, but he was perfect for her. He saw all the places she was broken, and he had confidence that she could fix them herself.

"I want to be your wife." Her heart was beating so fast that she heard blood rushing through her ears. "I love you."

"Gorgeous, I love you, too."

Chapter 20

Charlie's phone vibrated against the worn nightstand on her side of the bed. They'd spent the whole night apologizing to each other with lips and hands and screaming orgasms that she was surprised hadn't woken the neighbors.

The grey light through the curtains in the postage stamp apartment told her it was just past dawn. She looked over at her man, sleeping next to her where he belonged, and her heart filled and overflowed with the love she felt for him. He looked peaceful and hadn't woken from the noise.

Wanting to leave him that way, she grabbed his phone and pressed the green button to connect.

"Charlie's phone." She kept her voice down to a whisper.

"Who's this?" The woman on the other end had a ragged voice. For a moment, Laura worried that this was where her happiness all came falling down. She wondered if she would only have one night of sublime happiness, of knowing she could have everything she'd ever wanted before having it all taken away. Her heart stopped until the voice on the other line said, "This is Charlie's mother."

She knew that Charlie didn't call his parents and they didn't call him, and she'd thought the job offer via magazine article from his father had been weird. So, this had to be very serious.

"This is his wife." She maneuvered her way out from Charlie's arm and swung her legs off the bed so she could take the rest of the call in the bathroom. Feeling a sudden surge of protectiveness, she wanted to cut Charlie's mother at the pass if she was calling to cut him down. No one was allowed to do that anymore.

"It's his father." There was a muffled sob. "He's had a heart attack."

"I'm so sorry." She put her hand over her breast bone, rubbing the anticipatory ache that formed there at those words. Although they weren't close, there'd been something in Charlie's voice when he talked about his family—something unfinished. The thought that he wouldn't have the opportunity to make peace had tears springing up in her eyes. "Is he—"

"He's in the ICU. I just think—it might be a good idea for Charlie to come home." Another jagged breath. "Just in case it doesn't turn out."

Laura opened the bathroom door to find Charlie there. She held out the phone to him, wishing there was some way to soften the blow she was about to land. "It's your mother. Your father is in the hospital."

The face that had been restful in sleep moments ago, creased into a stressed out place she didn't want for him. He took the phone from her, and she moved to pass him in the small corridor, but he snaked one arm around her waist and crushed her to his body when he began speaking.

She stood there with him, holding him tight while he got the details from his mother. It was a short conversation, with him agreeing to get on the first flight. When it was over, he pulled away from her slightly.

"I hate to do this, but I have to go."

Laura shook her head and elevated onto the balls of her feet to kiss his cheek. "Of course you do."

He opened his mouth as though he was about to say something, but closed it before anything came out.

She turned to look for her phone. "I just have to call Matthieu to get the understudy in."

"You're coming with me?" His voice sounded shocked.

She stopped separating his clothes from hers on the floor, and stood straight. "How could I not go with you?"

"But the show—"

"I couldn't give a fuck about the show." She felt light saying that because it was true. "You need me in Chicago with your family, you have me."

Despite the dire situation, a smile lifted Charlie's whole face. "You love me."

"I told you last night." She pulled a sports bra over her head. Although she would have liked time to shower, a heart attack was serious, and they didn't have time to waste. "Didn't you believe me?"

"I did, but I don't want you to have to give up anything."

That did it. She crossed the room to him and wrapped her arms around his neck. "I'm going to have to be more convincing then."

She met his mouth with hers for a sweet kiss, something neither of them would be tempted to take further. Once she pulled back, she squeezed his shoulder. "Get dressed. I think I heard you say something about a private plane."

* * * *

Walking down the corridor in the cardiac intensive care unit was different that walking through the nursery and maternity care unit. Where those hallways were filled with infant cries and hopes, the beeping machines and cold hallway here spoke of death.

Charlie wished, with everything in him, that his father was one of the people here that was going to get well. If he didn't, if Joe's heart was too damaged to be repaired, there would always be something missing. In his twenties, he'd believed that he and his father would make up someday—that he'd have the chance to earn his respect.

Walking down the hall, Laura clutching his hand and lending him her unconditional support, he didn't care about respect. He just wanted the chance to show his father that this woman had seen him and found him worthy.

They walked up to the desk and found out that his father had gotten out of surgery and was resting. Only one of them was allowed in the room at a time, and his brothers had all taken their turns.

His mother was leaving the room, arms wrapped around her waist to ward off the chill of the ward, when they made it to his room. He hugged his mother. "How is he?"

Her snort surprised both him and Laura. "He's going to be fine. When we came in, they just rushed him in back, and I was terrified. But they stabilized him while you were in the air. Won't be able to drink as much scotch, but he's going to be fine." Relief washed through Charlie while his mother's attention lighted on Laura. "You're Laura."

"Yes, I am." That earned Laura a hug that shocked her, judging from the wide-eyed glare she leveled at Charlie. "You're my mother-in-law."

On the plane, they'd decided not to tell anyone in his family that they'd only had a sham marriage. They were planning on making it real—in private and totally sober—very soon. And, given recent cardiac events, none of the Laughlins needed a shock right now.

"Go on in," his mother said. "I'm going to take Laura to meet the rest of your hooligan brothers."

Laura grabbed his hand again. "I'm going to wait outside the room, I think." She gave him a look. "I want to meet them with Charlie."

He nodded and kissed her on the cheek, needing some of her steel to go in that room, hating that he had to leave her outside.

Charlie was shocked when he saw his father sitting up in bed, only attached to five or six machines. He had his reading glasses perched on his nose. And, if he weren't wearing a hospital gown and attached to the aforementioned machines, he might have been sitting in his office.

"Don't tell me you're here to apologize."

The statement felt like a slap across his face, but he recovered. "I have nothing to be sorry for right now. I'm here because you had a heart attack, and you're my father."

"I always knew you were too weak. I'd bet you let that pretty ballerina walk all over you."

Charlie actually jerked that time. He tamped down his rage because yelling at a bedridden man would be stupid.

"I can't believe you had a heart attack." Laura had come in the room, probably lingering closer than she was technically allowed under hospital regulations. "You seem pretty heartless."

"Laura—" From the red in her cheeks to the clenched fists, her anger was palpable. His father's words hurt, but they weren't something to go to war over. Although, part of him felt warmed that she was willing to throw down for him.

"No. He doesn't get to do this." Laura turned to him and grabbed his biceps. "He had angioplasty. He's only in the ICU because he's a VIP." That last acronym was swimming in criticism. "Your mother panicked."

"And he came running." His father let out a burst of laughter. "Wish I could get a fucking cup of coffee in here."

Laura turned back on his father. "You." She pointed a finger at him, but stayed at Charlie's side. "You need to stop. Do you think you have forever to fix this BS with your son? He's a good man. The best. He is brilliant, but I'm sure you've never even seen one of his programs."

"Now, young lady—"

Laura made a cutting motion with her hand that silenced his father. "Enough. I am so glad that Charlie got away from you. I don't tell him what to do." That was the truth. He'd never listened when she'd tried to push him away, and with her standing at his side, he was so glad that she hadn't. "He makes beautiful television, and he has a wonderful home. He's made a family, which I am so lucky to be a part of. And you don't care about any of it."

"I didn't say that."

Again, Laura cut him off. "Shut up. We were making up after our first fight, and that got interrupted. Unless you have a second surgery to actually install a soul, I think we're done here."

His father didn't respond. No one ever stood up to him. Even Charlie. As much as he'd wanted his father's approval, he'd never thought to demand it. But Laura saw things differently. She saw his father as the one who had something to lose by not being in Charlie's life. And, maybe, he could see himself through Laura's eyes.

There was nothing left to say, but Charlie needed to let one last thing sit with his father. "You know, I've spent my whole life waiting for you to approve of anything that I did. I didn't realize that your approval was meaningless until now."

And that was the truth. Laura had made him see that the only approval he needed was his own. And hers. He may not be able to survive without hers.

With that, she pulled on his arm and they left the room. They were halfway to the elevator and away from his whole family, when he pushed her into an empty room.

"What was that?" He couldn't help but lay a kiss on her mouth.

She smiled at him when he pulled back. "I'm just cranky because I haven't had a shower, and I had to meet your mother with sex hair."

"No, it wasn't. You stood up for me." This gorgeous woman was a warrior. Even last night, after they'd both laid everything out, he'd been worried that he'd pushed her into being with him. Her standing up for him made it clear that he was her choice, as much as she was his.

"Of course I did." She held his face with both her hands. "You're my sham, but soon-to-be-real husband."

He kissed her again. "Do you want to meet the rest of my family?"

"With sex hair?"

"It's not messy." He ran his fingers through it. "I could fix that, though."

She laughed as he backed up to close the door.

Epilogue

His wife was wearing a backless maxi dress. Everyone in the room knew she wasn't wearing a bra. Aside from making his pants uncomfortable, it made him want to kick her family out of his goddamned house so he could take her to the marble floor on her hands and knees.

She'd turned him into a barbarian, and she knew exactly how she was doing it. Even made sure her back was to him most of the time so he had no choice but to think about licking up her spine before slamming inside her. Every few minutes, she'd look at him over her shoulder. Sometimes she'd wink at him.

Asking for trouble. Before daylight, she'd find it.

But first, he had to host a fucking barbecue.

Jonah was standing next to him, giving instructions and motioning with his beer. "You're going to burn the food man."

"Do you want to do this?" Maybe if his friend manned the grill, he could drag his wife into their bedroom and give her a sliver of a taste of the kind of riding she was looking for.

His friend scoffed. "You're the grill master at your house. I'm the grill master at mine."

"Then shut the fuck up."

"You were a lot nicer before you got married."

"You were a lot more useful before you had a bunch of kids."

Carla had been pregnant with twins, and this was technically a baby shower. But the babies had been a little early, so they were here, too. Luckily, both little girls were perfectly healthy. His best friend was now thoroughly and irrevocably outnumbered. And not ready to return to the show anytime soon.

That was fine, because he wanted to pull back and focus on producing from Miami. He'd hire people to do the heavy-lifting and travelling.

Charlie sought out his wife again. She had her back turned, but her head was bent toward the little bundle in her arms.

He liked seeing her with a baby, but the twins and Layla were the only children she was likely to be holding for the next few years. And he was fine with that. He wanted her to leave ballet not because he was pressuring her to start family but because she was done with it.

After the production in New York ended, they'd offered her a place as a principal dancer. Charlie hadn't said anything other than, "This is your call. If you want it, I'll rent work space and find us an apartment."

Ultimately, she'd decided that she wanted to be at home in Miami. The Miami City Ballet had saved her from a shitty home life as a teenager, and she wanted to finish her career there.

Her brother Max stole one of the babies from her, which surprised Charlie. He hadn't taken Max for a baby person. But Laura was finding out a lot about her brothers now that they were all talking again.

Charlie got the last of the food off the grill, and said to Jonah, "Get everyone to make plates. And make sure Joaquin hasn't completely overrun the kitchen."

Laura's oldest brother didn't really like parties that he wasn't working at. So, he worked even at family parties. Whatever worked for him.

Bone deep satisfaction hit him when Laura wrapped an arm around his waist and rested her head against his shoulder. He loved this woman more than he'd ever thought possible. For him, their marriage had been real even when it wasn't. Because what they had had always been real.

After the last guests, Lola and Rogelio, left in the car he'd called for them, he found his wife cleaning up the kitchen. He kissed the back of her neck, and pulled her into the living room. He wanted to look at the light of the water reflecting against her skin.

Now that they were alone, he wanted to bend his wife over the back of their couch and claim her like she'd been signaling him to all day.

"You're a temptress."

"Why do you say that?" She squealed when he bit the tendon between her shoulder and neck.

"A siren." He moved her hair and tongued the sensitive skin behind her ear. "You know how I feel about you not wearing a bra."

"I forget sometimes." He savored the sound of laughter and lust on her voice. He would make sure she sounded like that at every opportunity for the rest of his life.

"Then, I'm just going to have to show you." They both stopped talking as he kissed every inch of herself she'd left exposed.

When he finally pulled her dress up and found her without panties, soaking and ready for him, he laced his hands through her hair and pulled her to him for a kiss. She burned him alive with her passion more and more each day.

As he thrust inside her, and she met him with every thrust, frantic and panting for release, he saw all of her. And loved every bit.

The End

Meet the Author

Andie J. Christopher writes edgy, funny, sexy contemporary romance. She grew up in a family of voracious readers, and picked up her first Harlequin romance novel at age twelve when she'd finished reading everything else in her grandmother's house. It was love at first read. It wasn't too long before she started writing her own stories—her first heroine drank Campari and wore a lot of Esprit. Andie holds a bachelor's degree from the University of Notre Dame in economics and art history (summa cum laude), and a JD from Stanford Law School. She lives in Washington, DC, with a very funny French Bulldog named Gus. Please visit her at andiejchristopher.com.

CPSIA information can be obtained
at www.ICGtesting.com
Printed in the USA
LVHW04s1551130818
586831LV00001B/191/P